D1058168

how
to
make
out

Also by Brianna Shrum
Never, Never

how to make out

Brianna R. Shrum

Sky Pony Press
New York

Visit our website at www.skyponypress.com.

10 9 8 7 6 5 4 3 2 1

Library of Congress Cataloging-in-Publication Data is available on file.

Cover design by Brian Peterson
Cover photo credit iStock

Print ISBN: 978-1-5107-0167-0
Ebook ISBN: 978-1-5107-0168-7

Printed in the United States of America

For Bnikholq (alias: Nicole), my April

Contents

OCTOBER

1. HOW to DO LONG DiViSiON

I prefer classrooms I can't set on fire. Not that I've started a slew of classroom fires in the recent past, but if I have to pick between solving for x or setting off the smoke alarms in home ec, I'm going with the numbers. So while everyone else is stirring batter the teacher constantly refers to as "beautiful," I'm chewing a whole finger off and praying to the culinary gods that somehow this gel in front of me will transform into a cake.

Mr. Cole harrumphs as he hurries past me. Like he's afraid if he lingers, my cooking-AIDS will infect him and he will be banished to the woodshop forever.

"That is Jell-O," someone says beside me.

I frown, but don't turn my head. "Thanks."

"I'm just saying, if you're trying to get a passing grade, that's not the way to do it."

My teeth grind against each other. "I'd like to see you do better." I rip my eyes away from the substance that can only be described as gloop and turn to face my heckler.

He raises an eyebrow and my mouth goes totally dry, so what comes out next is pretty much a croak. "Oh. Seth, right?"

This is a ridiculous thing to say. We've talked here and there in class; it's obvious I know who he is. But he nods, pretending he thinks my question is serious.

"So you probably *did* do better," I say under my breath, and he chuckles. Of course he did. Seth Levine could blink at raw eggs and flour and turn them instantly into a three-tiered feat of caketacular engineering. (And he could probably blink at just about any girl in the school and turn her instantly naked. Myself included. I've had this terrible low-level crush on him from afar since like the ninth grade.)

"It looks . . . salvageable."

I laugh out loud. "Is that what you'd call it?"

"You just need, like, two more cups of flour." He reaches for a bag across the table and rips it open. "And maybe—"

I snatch the bag away from him. "Thanks. But I think I can make a *cake*."

He rolls his eyes (his beautiful brown eyes) and steps backward, holding up his hands in a mock gesture of surrender. "Bake away. Sorry I said anything."

I snort and turn back to my bowl, annoyed at the flour. But he's right. So I tip the bag, and a steady stream flows into the . . . fine, Jell-O.

I hear the tiny sound of doom before I see it. A rip. And the whole thing tears. A flood of white powder assaults the bowl and puffs up in a cloud, coating the entire table. I just stand there, holding the empty bag, blinking at the bowl, which used to be green.

From the corner of my eye, I see Seth snickering and tapping his flour-coated fingers on the counter. I look over at him and sigh.

"You win," I say. "And I'm going to fail. I have a 98 percent in freaking calculus, but I'm going to fail *cooking*."

He narrows his eyes and glances over my shoulder. I follow his gaze and see Mr. Cole making his way through the rows of students, marking a piece of paper as he goes. This is it.

When I turn back around, the bowl in front of me is . . . green. And the batter is perfect. I blink at it several times and think for a moment that maybe the cooking gods have heard my plea. But then I see Seth's bowl, looking suspiciously white and flour-mountain-laden. I shoot him a look as Mr. Cole rounds the corner and he shakes his head minutely.

"Renley," I hear behind me. The way Mr. Cole says my name is similar to the way one would say "sewer rat." I turn and stare up at him, holding out my green bowl like a peace offering.

"Oh!" he says and smiles, scribbling on his paper. "Beautiful!" Of course it's beautiful. "Perhaps, Miss Eisler, baking is where your heart truly lies."

I blink, trying to avoid looking at Seth, who is barely holding back a snicker. "I—yes. Cakes and pastries are my passion."

"Mmhmm." He takes a step farther and raises an eyebrow at Seth. "Mr. Levine. What have we here?"

"Broken flour bag. I'm much better friends with a skillet than a mixing bowl, sir."

"Apparently." He jots down a few things but keeps a pleasant smile on his face. No sense upsetting the only culinary wizard in his class, I'm sure.

When he scuttles out of earshot, I lean over and whisper, "You didn't have to do that. I could have handled it."

Seth laughs and stirs the flour clump absently.

"I mean, I would have failed. But . . . well . . ."

"You're welcome," he says, grinning.

I roll my eyes.

"Really, though, I have ulterior motives," he says quietly.

My heart thumps suddenly and wildly. Is he kind of hitting on me? Is this flirting? This is totally flirting.

"Oh yeah?" I say. "What are those?" *Keep your sentences short. Don't say anything stupid.*

"Well, I figure since I helped you out, you might be able to help me out with something."

My mind comes up with all manner of dirty responses as he reaches into his backpack. He pulls out a folded piece of paper and sets it on the desk. I'm trying not to hope for some sort of Check Yes or No scenario while he unfolds it.

And it's . . . a trig paper. With an unimpressive number circled in red at the top.

"You're into math." It's not a question, just a statement under the guise of being one.

"Yeah."

"See, I just—"

I can feel myself relax almost immediately as I scan the numbers. Shoulders fall, head clears. Here. Here is my nirvana. "I see your problem right now. Your formula's off. A-squared plus b-squared equals c-squared, not c."

He just blinks at me. I'm surprised I'm not naked, given my prior theory on the Seth-blinking-at-a-girl thing. I point at something he's scrawled at the top. "See? C should be 4, not 16. 16 is c-squared. And 4 is the root."

"Ohhh," he says, taking the paper back. "So like, this one would be 7."

"You got it," I say with a smile that is surprisingly laid back, given the person I'm smiling at. But math is magic. To me, anyway.

He grins and tucks it back into his backpack. "You're good at this. You should tutor or something."

I nod. "Yeah, maybe." While I'm busy trying to discern if a conversation involving tutoring and the Pythagorean Theorem can *possibly* be construed as flirtatious, Mr. Cole signals for us to stick our bowls in the refrigerators lining the room and clean up. So that ends that musing.

A couple uneventful minutes later, the bell rings, and I head out with the throng of students into the hallway just in time to see Seth throw his arm around his ten-foot-tall Barbie of a girlfriend and saunter away.

He was not hitting on me.

Thankfully, I don't have much time left to embarrass myself with flirting/not flirting since school is over and the halls are rapidly emptying. I lean up against the wall, running a hand through my hair, attempting to rid it of what I'm sure is a coating of flour. I clutch my backpack to my chest, waiting for April to show.

She prances through the hallway and links her arm through mine, straight black hair swishing just below her chin, and I swing my backpack over my shoulder.

"Did you see this?" She thrusts a powder blue sheet of paper in my face and I have to stumble back just to get far enough away to read it.

"Math Club: NYC Trip." There is a light pang in my chest at the mention of New York, but I force it down and fake-smile at April. It's something she would usually catch, but she's crazy-excited. She snatches the flyer back and gestures so wildly, I have to duck every five seconds for fear she'll slash my face open with paper cuts.

"Yes! It's going to be *so awesome*. The Hayden Planetarium, the Museum of Mathematics, a couple college tours. And then, you know, the regular touristy things. Statue of Liberty, Empire State Building . . ."

Gag. On the one hand, yay, New York. On the other, my mom lives there with her new beautiful and perfect uber-family. And no thank you.

I swallow down the conflict playing out in my head and say, "It sounds fantastic. And expensive. It's $3,000."

"So you do the fund-raiser."

I shake my head. "Yeah. That'll about cover the cost of the in-flight meal. I can't do it."

And I'm not entirely sure I can hack the thought of going to New York, and being 96 percent sure Mom won't take a couple hours out of a day to see her estranged offspring. But also, yeah, money.

She frowns and starts to power-walk toward the door. "You could at least consider it," she huffs. "Don't just shoot it down after five seconds."

"April, come on. My dad's not a lawyer; you know that. He can't pay for this."

She slows down a little and pushes open the front door. Then she sighs. "I know. It's just, I don't want to do this trip at all if my best friend's not gonna be there. You have to at least *think* about it."

I sigh.

"Fine," I say, more to get her off my back than because I'm actually considering it. Drew is waving at me from the sidewalk, so I give April a quick hug and run off. I don't slow down when I reach Drew; he just starts running beside me.

"Survive Cole?" he asks.

"Barely."

Our feet pound against the pavement. His lope is easy, more of a jog than a run, and mine is hurried. I have to take two times the steps he does to keep up.

"Hear about New York?"

"Yeah. April's begging me to go."

He hesitates. "You going to?"

Heavy breathing between every stilted sentence.

"Doubt it." I rub my fingers against each other in the universal moneybags signal, and he nods, a little furrow in his brow he only gets when he's thinking hard. We run the rest of the way in silence.

By the time we get to his house, we're both dripping with sweat. His hair is sticking to his forehead and the back of his neck, and I'm sure mine is equally attractive.

"Coming in?"

I lean forward and put my hands on my knees, breathing in and out. "Sure."

After a minute or two, I straighten and follow him in through the front door.

"Mom's still at work," he says with a wink.

I roll my eyes and head into his room. We've lived next door to each other for ten years and have never been anything more than friends. But one errant eleven-year-old kiss down by the creek and he's still convinced it's going to happen again.

"I'm gonna go have a shower," I say. "I'm completely disgusting. And no, you can't join me."

"Go for it." He strips off his shirt and falls back onto his bed, reaching for his earbuds.

"Can I borrow a T-shirt?"

"I'll get one for you. And I think you left these here the other day." He holds up a skanky pair of pink shorts I'm certain aren't mine. I shake my head.

"Not yours?" He grins devilishly. "Well. Someone else's then. They'll fit."

"And *that*, Drew, is precisely why I'm never letting you join me in the shower."

He laughs. "You'd never let me touch you even if it weren't for all my . . . extracurricular activities."

"Fair enough."

8

I head into his bathroom and close the door behind me. Every time I'm in here (which is approximately every day), I'm distinctly reminded that it is a boy's bathroom. Mildew on the shower curtain. Toothpaste stains all over the sink. But the shower is clean enough to rinse off the sweat.

I strip down and hop in, coating myself in boy body wash and combination shampoo/conditioner I know can't be doing great things to my hair. When I get out, I smell pretty much exactly like Drew. He's left his over-sized band T-shirt and the short shorts on the toilet for me.

I slip on the shorts and pull the shirt on over my head. It's so long, you can't really see the shorts beneath the hem. Drew won't mind. In a way.

A prickle of guilt sticks my stomach and I wait in the bathroom for just a breath. He says he doesn't care, that it's fine. And what's the alternative? Stop hanging out with the only constant in a life of nothing but variables just because he's noticed I have boobs? No. Neither of us wants that. He says it's fine.

I head out into his room and sit next to him on the bed. He looks away for a second.

"What?"

"Get under the covers."

"Excuse me?" I ask, brows raised.

He stares back at me. "I cannot handle looking at you wet, in my T-shirt, with your legs looking like that. Get under the covers. I'll stay on top of them. I swear."

I don't say a word. I can't, without making it more awkward than it already is. So I do as he asks, prickle of guilt turned into a full-fledged flood. He flips on the TV to something stupid—*The Twilight Zone*, like always, and leans back, putting his arm around me.

"So," I say, eager to change the topic from my legs, "your mom still with—"

"Nope. New guy. He'll stay over tonight probably."

"We'll just turn the volume up when she gets here then," I offer.

He chuckles, in a way that is darker, I think, than he intends it to be. "Yeah. That'll help."

We sit there for a while, watching dumb stuff on TV, not really talking. At one point, he goes to the kitchen and heats up some Chinese food, which we eat together on the bed. After a few hours, it's dark.

"The whole New York thing?" he says.

"Yeah?"

"I think you should go."

"Why?"

"It'd be good for you. Get some school spirit and stuff," he laughs. I punch him. "Seriously, you should."

I stare straight ahead at the stupid TV show, trying to keep the emotion from my voice. "I don't know."

He's quiet for a minute. Then, "Her? You don't want to see her?"

"I don't want to *not* see her."

We lie there side by side, my head on his arm, and he shifts and kisses me on the top of my head. "Sucks."

"Whatever," I say.

"But you're gonna let a dickhead parent stop you from going to New York? April will kill you."

I laugh. I know. "Even if it weren't for my mom, I can't afford it, Drew," I say, laying my head on his bare chest.

"Eh, you're resourceful. You'd come up with something. If you really wanted to."

I think about it for a while. The emotional sucker punch I'm guaranteeing myself by going to the place my Deadbeat Mom lives, just to get blown off when I'm there because she can't look at me without thinking of Dad—that would blow. But I'm basically used to it by now, and Times Square . . . I'd kill to see Times Square. Plus, seriously, April's head would explode if I didn't at least try.

Maybe I will try. Just, like, without a firm commitment. But what can I do, really?

Tutor. You're good at that.

I cock my head, considering. "Maybe I'll start a blog."

"Random."

"No, like, what if I started a blog, like a paid thing?" I sit up, and fiddle with the edge of the blanket so it rests just past my knees. Drew purses his lips and looks away. I let go of it and it slides back down my thighs and settles at my waist. "Like, a how-to thing. People say I'm a good tutor." People. By people, I mean one person ever. "People could send in questions and stuff and I'll answer for a dollar or something."

"Workin' for dolla' bills. I never thought I'd see the day," he teases, shaking his head in fake disgust.

11

"Seriously though. It could maybe earn me something."

"Why don't you just pick up a part-time job? Bunch of places at the mall are hiring."

I shrug. "I don't know. I mean, I don't have a car, which would be kind of a major pain. Plus taxes? If I can do it this way, it'd be easier, I think."

"Sure. Why not?"

He relaxes again, so I lie back on him and focus on the TV.

I wake up in his bed, which is only surprising because I had no idea I'd fallen asleep. It's early, and it's Saturday, so I feel no need to rush next door to my house. It's not like Dad or Stacey will care, since I'm here more often than home. Instead, I tiptoe over to his computer, shaking my head at myself. This does *not* mean I'm going for sure.

But I start typing anyway: How to Do Long Division.

2. How to Deal With Your Best Friend's Extremely Awkward Mother

I hit PUBLISH just as Drew wakes. He sits up, bed creaking slightly, and scruffs his hair, smiling sleepily. "Hey there, beautiful. So, was last night as good for you as it was for me?"

I spin around slowly in the office chair and roll my eyes. "Go back to sleep."

He laughs and throws his feet over the side of the bed, body conspicuously absent of clothes.

"Hey," I say, indignant. "How come I have to hide my legs under the covers, but you can walk around the room in nothing but your boxers?"

"Three reasons." He heads into the bathroom and turns on the faucet. He's quiet for a second and emerges with his dark hair wet and dripping, rubbing a towel on his head. That so does not count for a shower, but I'm pretty sure in boy world, it does.

"One," he starts, rummaging through his closet, "this is my room. My rules." Fair enough. "Two, you're breaking the rules anyway, and I'm pretty sure I can actually see your underwear from here. No, no, don't get up."

I flush and switch positions as quickly as possible. He pulls a clean shirt over his head, which is actually slightly regrettable. I'm not about to get involved with him, but his chest was sculpted by the gods.

"And three, I could stand in front of you, modeling in my underwear all day, and never once would it cross your mind that you wanted to sleep with me. Bad. So bad you could taste it. 'Cause you're not in love with me." He says this all in a matter-of-fact way. It's so out in the open by now that that's the only way he *could* say it.

I swallow hard, looking away, and search the area around the desk for a blanket.

"And you definitely wouldn't be beating yourself up 'cause you couldn't stop imagining me naked."

My fingers find a thin cover and tug it up over my lap. Blood rushes to my cheeks.

He grins. "You're totally imagining me naked now, aren't you?"

I cough and shake my head. But now I am. It's like if someone says, "Don't think of a duck!" What's the first thing you think of? A duck.

He spins around slowly and holds him arms out, wiry muscles flexing. "Like what you see up there?" He taps his head.

"Drew!" I shriek. I wad up the blanket and throw it at his chest.

He catches it and heads over to the computer, pulling up the other chair right beside me.

"Come on, you know you don't have to worry about me. I'm not going to jump you the second you show a little leg."

"I know." I smile at him, feeling a little thrum in my chest I really do not want to feel, and then turn back to the computer screen.

"What do we have here?" he says, leaning over my shoulder.

"Nothing. Just a blog. Like we were talking about."

"So you're going then? To New York?"

I shake my head. "Maybe. I'm not committing to anything, though."

He clenches his jaw for just a fraction of an instant, then smiles, but it doesn't quite reach his eyes. "Yeah. You and your commitment issues."

I stiffen, but my pulse spikes. Focus on the computer screen.

He clears his throat. "So. How to Do Long Division."

"Yeah," I say, glad for the broken silence, but also feeling sheepish for some reason.

"Don't be embarrassed. You have a pretty good numbery explanation there. I'm just wondering how you plan to make money from it."

"Well, I figured it out this morning. I think my dad could probably cover a few hundred bucks. And fundraising, that'll cover another few hundred. With spending money and everything, I think I'll need about $2500.

And I have, like, seven months to do it." I quickly add, "You know. If I decide to go."

He raises an eyebrow. "Okay. And how is a free blog going to get you there?"

"I thought I'd leave it free for a little while, just answering questions from top Google searches and stuff. And putting up paid ads, of course. Then, when it gets a little more popular, I'll open it up to questions people can ask. But before the question goes up on the blog, they have to pay for it. And everyone else has to pay to access the answer."

"So, like all the free sites out there. Except you have to pay money."

I narrow my eyes. "No. I'm advertising that every answer comes from a certified expert."

He laughs. "Can you do that?"

I shrug. "I figure, why not? I'll just become an expert on whatever, and it'll be true."

"Huh. Might as well give it a shot."

I turn his chair to face mine. "You can't tell *anyone*."

He furrows his brow. "Why not?"

"Because, the success of this whole thing depends on anonymity. Right now, I'm invisible. I'm not a loser, I'm not popular. I'm just . . . there. No one wants to pay for advice from me. I'm invisible in a lame way. I need to be invisible in, like, a *Gossip Girl* way."

"Okay, I got you. I vow my silence. Pinkie swear. Or should we do this in blood?"

I arch a brow. "I'm surprised you didn't want to seal it with a kiss."

"I wasn't going to say anything, but since you suggested it . . ." He leans forward and I slam my hand into his chest, knocking him backward. The chair flips over with a crash and he falls out of it into a small pile of dirty laundry.

My eyes go wide and I clasp my hands behind my back.

"So, that's how you like it then," Drew rasps. He just lies there for a second, blinking slowly.

I get out of the chair and reach out to him. "Uh, sorry. Don't know my own strength, and all that."

"Apparently." He takes my hand. As I'm attempting to pull him up, the door to his room opens. The smell of boy and Chinese food is instantly overpowered by cologne, alcohol, and strong perfume. All left over from last night, I presume. Drew's usually-put-together mom is a mess of unbrushed hair and smudged eyeliner.

"What is going on in—" She stops and smiles politely at me, giving me an obvious once-over. I'm even more conscious now that it looks like I've got nothing on under Drew's T-shirt. "Drew," she says, "you should put a tie on the door or something."

I don't think my skin has ever been a darker shade of crimson. "Hey, Ms. Calloway."

"Renley. Always good to see you."

The silence is palpable. And awkward. Even Drew isn't totally comfortable, which is an anomaly. He's staring at her, nose just slightly wrinkled, usually bright eyes embarrassed. And pissed. I wonder if he notices the hickey just above her left boob.

Ms. Calloway clears her throat and looks away. "Well then, I'll just, um, leave you to it."

She backs out and shuts the door quietly. Drew puffs out an embarrassed sigh and shakes his head, hard.

I glance at him. "Does she really not care if you have girls in here?"

He coughs. "Did you not see the giant hickey or smell that frat boy cologne? She doesn't have room to talk even if she did. And no. You know that."

I do. Still, it seems like it needs some sort of comment.

He smiles, then, wiping the ragey embarrassment from his face. "In all honesty," he says, almost laughing, "I think she'd be more concerned if she thought we *weren't* screwing."

"That is so messed up."

He shrugs and hands me my dirty clothes from yesterday. I take them into his bathroom and shut the door behind me. Few boundaries I refuse to cross in front of him, and actually getting naked is one of them. When I come out in my own crumpled clothes, he takes back his shirt and Random Girl's shorts.

"You probably ought to get back home before your dad gets pissed."

"Oh yeah, I'm terrified."

He grins. But he's right; I do need to go. Not because of my dad. Ever since he cheated on my mom (like *five years ago*) and they got divorced, he's got Divorced Dad Guilt about everything and lets me do literally whatever I want. With whomever I want. I'm sure he thinks Drew and I are sleeping together. But he never says a word about it, and my guess is he never will.

"I do need to go, though," I say.

"Yeah. I have some things I need to do anyway."

"What kind of things?"

"I have a hot date later."

I look slowly around the room. "And you're expecting her to come in *here*?"

"Who do you think you're talking to here?" he says, a little half-grin on his face.

"Well. You should . . . clean up. At least spray some air freshener or something. And hide those shorts."

"I do not need tips from you on how to get laid, little Renley. But thank you for the advice." He pushes me out the door and I half-smile, half-purse my lips.

"I'll see you later," I say, shaking my head.

"See ya. And if you come over tonight, text me first. But I doubt she'll be here past ten."

I close his door behind me and sneak out into the foyer. I'm not entirely sure why I feel the need to sneak; his mom has already seen us and assumed the worst, like, three hundred times. Still. It's weird.

"Renley?"

FATALITY.

"Hey, Ms. Calloway. Just heading out."

"Well, before you leave, take these." She drops several handfuls of something into my palms, and I don't even want to know what they are. Except I do know. They're condoms. A crap ton of condoms.

"Um." I have nothing else to say. What are you supposed to say when you're standing with your best friend's mom, in the middle of the kitchen, and hordes of likely flavored, neon-colored condoms are pouring from your hands?

"Don't be embarrassed. Just take them."

Ugh. Yeah. She was definitely playing the cougar role last night. Frat boy body spray is assaulting my nostrils.

I try to hold my breath. But I have to say something, because the bizarre *I'm the cool mom* conspiratorial look she's giving me is almost worse than the cologne. "Okay. I'm just not sure how else to say this, but I am not sleeping with your son."

She pats my shoulder. "Oh, honey. I wasn't born yesterday. Don't worry about it. Just take them. Be safe."

I'm not sure if I should look at her face or at the ground, or at all the latex in my hands. So I just look frantically among all three.

"But I'm really, honestly, *not*. I swear. I'm a vir—"

"Just take them, sweetie. Your secret is safe with me." She winks, which makes it all infinitely worse. I turn around, eyelids glued open, and make a move stiffly toward the door. Drew walks in, takes one look at my birth control–laden hands, and chokes on nothing. He brushes past me, bee-lining for his mom (but takes a condom as he walks past), and I open the door and let it slam behind me.

"MOM," I hear, muffled behind the door.

"What?" she says.

Seconds later, I get a text from him.

Dude. I don't even.

I write back,

It's fine. I'll just, like, make balloons or something.

White balloons? Lovely party.

They're all multicolored. And flavored.

Stop sending words. You're talking about my MOM'S condoms.

The screen darkens and I laugh, then head inside.

3. How to Do a Waterfall Braid

"Hey, Leelee," my dad says as I walk through the door. He's called me that since I was little. It's stupid, but I kind of love it.

"Hey, Dad."

"Where you been?"

"Drew's."

He forces a smile, like he always does after I spend the night next door. And he avoids looking at my face, like always. It's tough, I suppose, thinking your daughter is whoring it up with her hot, man-slut neighbor. I shift my weight back and forth, wondering for a split second if he'll say anything. If maybe, for once in the last five years, he'll Dad up and ground me or take my phone or *something*.

"Well," he says, voice stilted and clearly uncomfortable, "I'm, uh, glad you had fun with your friend."

He looks back toward the kitchen for a split second and takes a sip from his coffee mug, and I allow myself one head shake. One head shake of annoyance, and I don't even know why. Having the ability to go punishment-free on everything is a superpower, not a nuisance. But right now, it feels like one anyway.

He looks back at me (not at my eyes; he's avoiding those quite expertly), and his gaze flicks down to my hands. My hands, which are overflowing with condoms.

Oh no. Panic mode. What do I do with these? Can I tell him they're tiny candy packets? Hide them in my pockets? I hate Drew's mom. I hate her so much.

Dad spits out his coffee, like people only really do in the movies, and just stares.

"Wh—what are those?"

"Uh."

He gets up from the table and sets down his coffee.

"Renley, *what* are *those*?"

"Dad, I—" and I stop. Part of me wants to defend myself. To tell him I've never kissed Drew (fifth grade not included), let alone slept with him. Or anyone else, for that matter. To tell him Ms. Calloway is crazy and wouldn't let me leave until she'd buried me in a mountain of birth control. But the other part . . . the other part wants to lie. "They're condoms, Dad."

His jaw drops. There's nothing but silence, silence we can both really feel, for two minutes, minimum. And I'm the one who breaks it.

"What do you think I do at his house when I stay over?"

"I . . . I, uh . . ."

"Do you think we just sit there, watching movies all night and braiding each other's hair?"

"Renley—"

"I'm not eleven anymore, Dad."

His eyes dart around the room, at every single thing but me. And I just stand there, clutching the condoms. When he finally speaks, it's quiet. And tired. "You're right. You're not a child anymore. And . . . I'm sorry."

I bark out a laugh. "You're sorry."

"Of course I am. You're old enough to make your own decisions. And at least you're being safe."

I don't even know what to say to that. So I don't.

"He does have a lot of girls going in and out of there, Leelee. You need to be careful."

The door creaks open as I turn and start up the stairs.

"Hi, Leelee!" Stacey says brightly. "We missed you last night!"

I *hate it* when she calls me that. I ignore her and walk faster, disappearing into my room. I have no idea why I'm so pissed. I just am. I slam the door behind me (yet another thing my dad will refuse to punish me for) and whip out my phone.

Dad saw your mom's . . . gifts to me.

Was he pissed?

He didn't care. At all.

I feel kind of stupid about the whole thing now. About getting angry about my dad not ever getting angry. Why does it matter if my dad doesn't care about my fake sexual habits? The phone buzzes.

Well, you know, my mom wants me to put a tie on the door so she knows if I'm hooking up w/ someone lol

lol parents

I set the phone down on the computer desk, running a hand through my hair to chill myself out, and log in to my blog. Five views. Not breaking any records.

What else do I even know how to do, aside from math? I start typing in the search engine. How to . . . How to Boil Eggs? Really? There's no way that's the fourth highest search. Whatever, I can do that. One of the few things I can cook.

1. Add salt to water.
2. Add eggs to cold water.
3. Bring to boil.
4. Boil for 9 minutes.
5. Eat.

And find a way to make that interesting. Add a couple gifs, maybe.

PUBLISH.

I blink at the archive. "How to Do Long Division." "How to Hard Boil Eggs." This is the most boring blog on the face of ever. I scroll through some more search engine stuff for a while. "How to Do a Waterfall Braid." Interesting.

I plop myself in front of the mirror with several YouTube videos playing at once. Over, under, over, under. And nothing that resembles anything. I try many times (quite unsuccessfully) and by the end of this whole venture, my hair resembles the nest of a small bird.

I scramble for a hairbrush, trying to decide whether I need to deep-condition my hair first, or if that will just make it worse.

Someone knocks at my door. "Come in."

"Hi, honey."

"Hey."

Dad comes and sits on my bed. I ignore him and continue searching for a brush. Somehow, when he's here, I'm mad again.

"New hairstyle?"

"Ha. Kind of."

"Are you mad at me?" he asks, fiddling with his watch. Dad still wears a watch, even though he has a smartphone that can tell him the time in every time zone in the world.

I stare up at the poster of the periodic table on my wall. (I'm aware it is the nerdiest thing on earth.) Focus away from Dad, and on the numbers. Calm. "No."

"At Stacey?"

"No."

He sighs heavily. "Listen, I wasn't trying to hurt your feelings or embarrass you earlier. It's just, since your mom lives six hundred miles away, and is well, you know . . . I know you don't get the chance to really talk about this kind of stuff, you know, sex stuff, with anyone. And you're growing up. You have needs now."

"*Dad*, oh my gosh."

"No, hey, it's fine. I was a teenager once. I understand. And your hormones are going crazy and all you can think about is . . . jumping someone's bones."

"Seriously. Stop."

"I just wanted to let you know that it's normal. And you're not a slut or anything. But I need you to know that you could get pregnant if you're not being safe. Every time. And a boy like Drew is sleeping with *a lot* of girls. And you could get chlamydia."

"Drew does not have chlamydia, okay?"

I want to crawl . . . not under my covers. That's not hidden enough. Into my mattress. That's where I want to be right now.

"Well, sweetie, he could, and he wouldn't know it. Or gonorrhea."

All of a sudden, making my dad believe I'm having sex with Drew is not as appealing as it was fifteen minutes ago. He's not going to punish me for it anyway, or act pissed, even. So what am I enduring this for? "Dad, stop. Seriously. I'm not sleeping with him. Those condoms were from his insane mom, and I'm not. I'm a virgin. I don't have chlamydia."

He sits back a little, looking more uncomfortable, somehow. "Oh. Well. Alright then. But you know you can get STDs from other stuff too. Like—"

"I *know*, Dad. Thank you for this talk. I'm sure it's prevented me from having a wealth of children and contracting a medical journal's worth of diseases. This has been very meaningful. Please, go downstairs."

"Well, if you ever need to talk . . ."

"Yes. You will be the first one I call."

Now. Since Mom no longer answers her phone for me.

I practically push him out the door. But then I remember the New York thing.

"Dad?"

The look on his face when he turns around is so full of dread, I would laugh if I wasn't totally mortified, too.

"The Math Club is going to New York in seven months. And I could use some money for the trip. I'm thinking about going."

He breathes out a relieved sigh and the look of terror flees his face. "How much?"

"The trip is $3,000. But I'm saving most of it myself. I just need to know what you could help with."

"I'm not sure, honey. Let me talk to your mom."

I shoot him a look. He and Stacey are always trying to pull that. Like just because Mom can't bring herself to acknowledge me, Stacey is now the woman who birthed me.

"Stacey," he corrects himself. "We'll be able to help you out." He turns to leave and then takes a step backward. "Is Drew going?"

I roll my eyes. "Drew's not into math. I'm going with April."

He smiles easily. "Good." Then he frowns. "New York? Like—"

"Yes, Dad. Like where Mom lives. I'm staying with her while I'm there."

The lie slips easily and strangely off my tongue. I don't even really know why I said it. But it gets this stunned, punched-in-the-gut reaction from Dad, like maybe he's going to forbid it. Or have a mild heart attack. It could go either way. Then he leaves on his own and shuts the door.

My dad thinks you have chlamydia.

Gross.

I twirl around in my chair for a while before dialing April's number. She picks up after one ring.

"Hello?"

"Okay. I'm going."

"To New York?" she asks, the pitch of her voice rising with every syllable.

"Yup." That reaction from Dad cemented it. I'm going.

She shrieks, and I hold the phone away from my ear, wincing.

"Oh my gosh. We have to plan out everything. This is going to be so perfect. And so awesome. And so, so . . . I'm so glad you're going!"

I smile into the receiver, though I know she can't see me.

"Me too. Can't wait to take on NYC with you, love."

Her older brother makes some obnoxious but muffled sound in the background and she yells something equally uninterpretable. Then there's a deafening tone in my ear. Disconnected.

I turn back to YouTube. Now that I've said it to April, it's real. I have to turn this blog into something readable, and if waterfall braids are the way to do that, I'm more than willing to put my hair through some abuse.

So I twist and twist and twist again. And at the end of the day, I slather a TON of Stacey's too-tan-for-me foundation on my hands and arms (super-secret disguise precautions) and snap a few pictures of the back of my head. Toss those in Photoshop to darken my hair a couple shades (yeah, a math geek who's good at computers. Surprise, surprise.), and bam. I've got it published.

And the final nail. I whip out my phone before I can think about it too hard and text Mom. I tell her I'll be coming up there from Ohio this summer and ask when we can hang out.

She doesn't respond right away, but she will this time. I know it.

4. How to Tie a Tie

Come over. I hit SEND. Then five seconds later, **Wait. You're not with a girl or anything are you?**

No. All's quiet over here.

Bring a tie.

;)

Possibly a dress shirt or something too.

That's less fun.

I flop back on my bed, scrolling through Google and the blog simultaneously. I haven't made a cent yet, but it's definitely going way up in views since last week. Guess waterfall braids are much more interesting than long division. "How to Do Cat Eyes." Ooh. That's a good one. And I figure if I steal one of Stacey's cobalt-blue colored contacts and just do uber-close-up shots of, like, one eye at a time, no one will suspect a thing.

I jump up and head over to my desk, which will have to double as a vanity for now. There's a mirror behind it, so it counts. I have to own at least one eyeliner pencil. Somewhere.

I dig through the second drawer, where all the remnants of the makeup I used to care about wearing in the ninth grade have gone to rest. And, eureka. One tiny stub of an eyeliner pencil. It's old. Possibly not completely hygienic. But it will do what it needs to do, which is, apparently, make me look like a cat.

I close my right eye and sweep the liner over my top lid. Simple enough. And just keep sweeping. I open it, expecting feline grace and beauty. Instead, I get half-a-Cleopatra. But my hair looks extremely waterfally, and freaking fantastic, so there's that.

I close my left eye, despite the failure, and try again. This time, it at least curves upward. But still, decidedly Old World Egyptian, not so much Modern Vixen.

There's a light knock on my door.

"Yeah," I call.

Drew walks in. I can't see him because I'm still focused on the terrible effort I've put forth in the makeup department, but I know it's him.

"Your hair looks nice," he says.

I spin around and smile, and he almost loses it.

"Whoa, Cher. I was looking for Renley. Clearly, I got the wrong room."

I choke on nothing. "I hate you."

I spin back around and pick up a Kleenex, wiping furiously at my maimed eyes. It leaves this kind of smudgy residue which actually looks nice, so I leave that and stand.

"How to Do Cat Eye Makeup," I explain.

"You might want to keep working on that before you publish."

"Thanks for the tip."

He half grins and sets down the bundle of clothes in his arms.

"So, the tie. I'm going to assume this has something to do with your blog. Either that, or this relationship is going in a *very* different direction than I thought."

I laugh. "The former."

He nods. "It is as I feared." And he sits on the bed next to the dress shirt and tie.

"I need to learn how to tie a tie."

"Easy enough."

I pull the tie out of the shirt sleeve and throw it around my neck, just letting it hang there, staring at myself in the mirror. "I have no idea how to go about this."

He comes up behind me and reaches around my shoulders, and I refuse to acknowledge the furious jumping of my pulse. "Just watch my fingers."

He moves them slowly, step by step, right side over the left, under, right over left again, and under again. After that, he loses me a little. We're not dating. We're *never* dating. But his fingers brushing against my throat, my collarbone, and his arms around mine, his chest pressed against my back—I can't think.

33

"You got that?" he says. His voice is low. Not because he's trying to be sexy, just because his mouth is so close to my ear. And knowing full well that he is not trying to seduce me makes it even sexier. This is ridiculous.

"I got the first part. After that, um . . . I, um . . ." My voice is cracking like crazy.

"You okay?"

"I'm *fine*, Drew. This is just not working at all," I snap, untangling the tie from my neck and throwing it at the bed. I take several steps back, till the edge of my desk is digging into my butt.

His eyebrows shoot up and he sits back on my bed, running his fingers nervously over the tie. "Uh, okay. Sorry?"

If he knew how fast my heart was going and the thoughts running through my head at this exact moment, he'd be backing to the other side of the room, too. (Maybe.)

"It's not you," I say, trying not to sound frustrated. "It's just . . . maybe I need to figure out how to do this on someone else first. Maybe that's easier."

"Sure. Okay." He's still super uncomfortable, fidgeting and awkward, and I feel a rush of guilt.

I stand up from the desk and take the tie back from him. "Sorry I freaked out a little."

"It's fine." He pauses, rubbing the back of his neck, then, "Did you want me to change or something?"

Oh yeah. The dress shirt. "I don't know. Is it different with the collar?"

"Not really. Maybe a little."

I nod. "Yeah, you might as well."

He peels his shirt over his head and reaches for the dress shirt he brought. Part of me feels uncomfortable at this second, seeing him shirtless. He's always been hot, but I'd rather not look at him while I'm all, what was it Dad said? Run by hormones? Needing to "jump someone's bones"?

That pretty much does it. I laugh out loud, and he just raises an eyebrow, but magically, I can look at his chest again without feeling things I don't want to feel.

He closes the shirt button by button, all the way to the top. I loop the tie around his neck and wait.

"Tuck it under the collar," he says.

I stand on my tiptoes so that I can reach around his neck. My chest is pressed against his, and I can see the pulse pounding beneath his jaw. Just like that, my magic bone-jumping solution dies.

"So the big side is on your left. Cross it over the little side."

I do as he says, then cross it under. And repeat.

"Good. Now, while the big side is still underneath everything, pull it up through the loop at the top. The one around my neck."

I pull it through, and my knuckles rest against his throat. I let my hand relax for just a split second, enjoying the feel of his skin on one side of my hand and the silk on the other.

"Um," he chokes out, not looking at me. "Uh, you're going to . . ." He swallows, and I feel his Adam's apple move against my hand. "You're gonna just pull it through the little loop now."

His voice is hoarse. And I'm pretty sure if I said anything right now, mine would be, too.

I move just a little closer to him, and my face is hardly an inch from his jaw. For once, I'm extremely aware of it. I transfer the tie from one hand to the other and pull it through.

"Then just tighten."

I'm not sure if he realizes that his voice has dropped to the point where it's nothing but a throaty whisper. I try to ignore it and tighten. Too tight.

His hands fly to his throat, and he loosens the tie quickly. "Not like a noose, R. You don't want to kill me." He smirks.

"Well, not at the moment."

"Fair enough."

Standing there, in jeans and a dress shirt and a loosened tie, he looks just the right kind of unkempt. Hot. So hot. Maybe this blog post was not exactly worth it.

"You wanna try again?" he asks.

No. "Sure."

And so we do. Several times, until I can get it looking halfway decent, and the little end doesn't stick out of the big one. It's actually looking pretty good.

"Wanna try one on yourself?" he says.

"Yeah." *But you're not touching me this time.*

He loosens the tie from around his neck and undoes the shirt, but leaves the tie on while he strips his shirt off. It would be stupid if he didn't look like a Hollister ad while he did it. But he takes the thing off eventually and pulls his old T-shirt back on and hands the tie to me. It doesn't take a ton of effort to convert what I've learned to tying my own tie. After another day or two, I can post the blog, I think.

"Mind if I keep this for a couple days?"

"Go for it. But don't wash it or ruin it or anything. Girls go crazy for a tie." He winks, and the spell is broken. Sometimes I forget that Drew wants to lay everything that moves. And it's fine. No judgment. But I've seen *that* before, and I know how the story goes when a damaged girl hooks up with a guy who can't keep it in his pants. And even though a big part of me wants to know what it would feel like to really kiss him, approximately zero part of me wants to end up like my parents. So he's hot. But not something I want to get involved in. Or will. Ever.

"Thanks," I say and flop back on the bed. I flick on the TV and turn to him. "So, *Twilight Zone?*"

He slides up to the pillow and throws an arm around me, and just like that, things are back to normal.

5. How to Get the Entire Math Club to Seriously Doubt Your Numerical Abilities

If I check my phone enough times, maybe my mom will transform into a legit parent. If I check it enough, maybe the little icon that says READ will disappear, and I'll discover it just hasn't been delivered. I check again.

"Renley," says April. She snaps in front of my face. "Renley. Hello?"

I blink dumbly and stare at the white board, working the equation in my head like lightning. "Uh. 6.784. Sorry."

April gives me a half-irritated, half-impressed look, and I try to stop fiddling with my phone and pay attention to the board. But after a second stupidly delayed response and half the club looking at me like they're wondering if I got whacked over the head with something heavy, I excuse myself and stumble into the restroom, glad that this was a student-led practice. If Mr. Sanchez saw me acting like a total moron, I think I would die a little.

I rub my hands over my eyes and stare down at my phone. READ. READ. READ. And no response for three days.

I get it. I get not wanting to have any kind of contact with the man who walked out on you for a twenty-five-year-old, perky version of yourself. And I get that I kind of remind her of him, or whatever. But I don't get going from watching old movies and painting our toenails and eating pizza and, honestly, having a relationship most of my friends were jealous of to not even putting up a fight for custody.

And I don't get never answering my calls or texts, or not even wanting to see me when I'm in town. Or on Christmas. I'm not the one who had sex with someone else.

Seriously, Bruce Willis and Demi Moore, when they got a divorce, they bought houses, like, next door to each other. Is that kind of parting of ways too much to ask for? I don't know. It doesn't really matter. I can complain about it all I want—I can call, text, cry—but it's not gonna change that little status taunting me. READ. READ. READ.

Tears sting my eyes and I wipe at them and suck it up. Vow to pay attention in math club. I allow myself a few unsteady breaths, then tuck in my lower lip and head out of the bathroom and into the mostly empty hallway.

"Whoa," says a voice I recognize. I almost run into him, and he reaches out to grab my arms, steady me.

"Oh. Seth. Sorry," I mumble.

He chuckles and pulls back from me, beautiful sun-bronzed skin no longer touching mine, which is a bit of a bummer. "It's fine," he says. Then he peers at me. "Hey, are you okay?"

I blink quickly, trying to rid my eyes of tear-evidence, but I'm kind of an ugly crier, so that's not gonna do much to dissipate the red blotches on my skin, which I'm sure are doing wonders for the small breakout I'm currently experiencing.

"I'm fine. It's nothing," I say.

He narrows his eyes. "You sure?"

I laugh nervously. "Yeah. It's just, you know, parent stuff."

He nods and leans back against the wall. "Yeah, I get it. Parents."

I nod, mimicking him and folding my arms. Then there's this odd, awkward silence. I reach for my phone because I'm not sure what to do with my hands.

"So, do you have somewhere to be?" he asks.

"Oh. Yeah. Math club." I am *so* cool.

"Cool," he says. See? There you have it.

He smiles and stands up straight. "I'll let you get back to math club, then. See you in home ec tomorrow?"

Then he walks away and I wave, and I just stand there for a second afterward, mouth hanging open. Typically our relationship consists of me waving an awkward greeting followed by a stream of syllables that only vaguely resemble "Hello," and him smiling and nodding at me, then walking away. I am so not used to this whole "interacting with Seth like two equal humans" thing. I'll take it, though.

After I gather myself, I walk off back to math, just in time to answer one more question and duck out with April.

"So," she says. "You, uh, okay?"

"Fine. Why?"

"You were being all distracted and bizarre," she says, linking arms with me.

"Yeah, it's just . . . mom stuff. Okay?"

April nods. She knows not to push me when it comes to certain things, this being one of them. We head outside to her brother's car. He's parked out front, windows down, blasting something from ten years ago.

Seth spots me from across the parking lot and raises his hand in a wave, and I smile and half wave back before I duck into the back seat of Keith's car. April raises an eyebrow at me, but I just say, "It's nothing," before we drive off.

"So. How was numbers, punk?" Keith asks with a bright smile. The sun is doing nice things to his white-blond hair. Moments like this, I'm often struck by the sharp difference between them. Keith is this tall, tan, clean-cut All American, where April's hair changes color every couple weeks, and she's tiny and pale and has more than one piercing in her face.

"Fine," says April. "Hey. Buy us some beer before we get home."

Keith laughs. "Right."

"Come on."

"Yeah. That's what I need on my record right now. Providing liquor to underage ladies. Can't do it. Not even for you," he says, shooting a glance back at me and winking.

I giggle and he grins. He's a fake flirt. Cute, but nothing more than April's older brother. And a pseudo-adoptive one to me. April heaves a sigh of long-suffering and I lean back in the seat. Keith does stop by a drive-through and gets us a couple malts to make up for it, though, which works fine for me. Beer tastes like crap anyway.

"Hey," he says to me when we pull up to their house and hop out of the car, "that dude you were waving to in the parking lot. He a Levine?"

"Yeah," I say. April side-eyes me. "Why?"

"No reason. Just thought I recognized him."

I frown. "How?"

"Oh. I just . . . I liked to hang out with his sister back in the day, from time to time." A wicked grin lights up his bright blue eyes.

April hits him with her backpack. "Gross, Keith!"

He holds his hands out in surrender and backs up, laughing. "No, it wasn't like that. Their family is super religious. We just made out a few times. No harm, no foul."

April rolls her eyes grandly and walks ahead of him, and I shrug, then follow her. He's still laughing when we go in. April pretends to still be disgusted, but then we all plop down on the couch together, and Keith tosses us both PlayStation controllers. We hang out and play *Call of Duty* for a while before I have to go home.

I don't check my phone while I'm there. Or my blog. I just chill and wonder if maybe, someday, Keith won't be the only one to have gotten to first base with a Levine.

6. How to Get Your Flirt On

It takes me a few days, but after several tragically maimed Pharaoh-esque makeup attempts, my cat eye efforts come to fruition. I actually look pretty put together this morning, more so than usual: hair in curls that are just this side of perfect, eyes that are actually highlighted by the bold makeup attempt. This may be the first time since early freshman year that I haven't shown up to school in a thrown-together ponytail and ChapStick.

I meet Drew outside my house, and he whistles when he sees me.

"It's almost a shame for us to run to school when you look like that."

I grin. "I'm not gonna lie to you. I look really sexy today."

"You'll get no arguments from me there." He flicks a glance from the top of my head down to my feet and back up again. "Yeah, we're taking my car."

Normally, I would protest. But for some reason, the idea of keeping this sudden hotness intact is appealing. So I go to his little car with him. I slide inside, head almost hitting the ceiling. It's clean in here, but with the distinct feeling of "old." Peeling silver paint on the outside, a ratty stick shift between the seats. The kind of car that keeps your adrenaline pumping the whole time you ride because you're not entirely sure the brakes won't give out. He could afford to trade up, but he doesn't. I've never figured out why.

"Checked your blog stats lately?" he asks as the car chokes and shudders to life. He jerks it into gear and we roll into the street.

"Not since last week."

"They're way up today."

My eyes widen in slight surprise, then narrow. "Is it because you've visited five hundred times in the last two days?"

He laughs and shifts and the car picks up speed. "No. I mean, I check up on it. Mostly to get some fabulous hair and makeup tips. But check them out. That little view tracker at the bottom of the page is going nuts. This whole thing might actually work."

I lean back and smile, pictures of the Empire State Building and Broadway flashing through my head. Screw Mom. New York will be amazing enough without her. When we get to school, I hop out of the car before he does, toss him a wave, and head off to calc with April. She links arms with me and chatters about my sexy makeup and New York, which is pretty unsurprising. And then she shoots a look back at Drew.

"Are you guys hooking up yet?" she asks.

"April," I say, rolling my eyes. She laughs and drags me through the doors and down the hall. We're in class way early, mostly because I rode to school.

"Hey Renley," says Mr. Sanchez. "Hear about the New York trip yet?"

"Of course."

"It should be pretty dope. Happenin'. All the cool kids are going."

I laugh out loud. Mr. Sanchez is the math club coach and pretty much everyone's favorite teacher ever. (Except the kids in remedial math, who hate anyone associated with numbers. But he never really had a chance there.)

"You gonna come?" he asks, pulling up a chair and sitting in it backward, facing April's and my desks.

I glance over at April, whose beaming face is giving away the answer. "Planning on it," I say.

"Awesome. I didn't think you'd send April here out into the concrete jungle by herself."

"It's the sacrifice a good friend has to make," April chirps, tossing her jet black bangs out of her face and grinning.

"Right," Sanchez says, raising an eyebrow. He gets up out of his chair and heads back to his desk, rustling his papers and getting into the "professional teacher position" before the rest of the kids show up.

April fiddles with her lip ring, twisting it around and around, and my teeth grind against each other as I watch her. Metal on teeth. Shudder.

"So," she says, leaning over onto my desk, "I had a date last night."

"You did?" I lean in closer to her. "With who?"

"Cash."

"And?"

"Movie was weird. So we made out through the whole thing. It went well."

"Was he good?"

She leans back in her chair and smiles. "Oh yeah."

Cash walks in seconds after. He's the stereotypical math geek: thick, square glasses, unkempt hair, smart. But, I have to admit, kind of charming. (And apparently a deceptively good kisser.) He steals a glance at April and turns back around, sitting in his chair, obviously trying to hide the spark. April and I laugh behind our hands at one another. If guys had any idea what girls knew about each other . . .

Calc today is stuff April and I could both do in our sleep. So I switch my calculator to keyboard mode.

Is Cash going to NY?

I slide it over onto her desk. Sly. Most kids only know that if you type in 8008 on a calculator, it spells BOOB. But if you have a fancier one, and you switch to keyboard mode, you can pass notes forever. If a teacher figures it out, you can delete the whole conversation in one keystroke. Most useful thing either of us ever learned in math.

She raises an eyebrow at the message, purses her lips.

Who cares? It's forever from now. We're barely an item even.

Fair enough.

I wanna go see Phantom, she writes.

Or Hamilton!

Or ooh, a sexy show. Strippers! Man thongs!

I laugh obnoxiously loud in the middle of Sanchez's lecture and he frowns at me. I erase the calculator. Now seems to be the appropriate time—snort-laughter, strippers, and man-thongs all considered.

The rest of calc drags on. After, April prances off to her next class, and I have a free period. Why I chose a free period right before lunch instead of after is beyond me, but at least I know the error of my ways now.

I slide down the wall in the empty hallway and turn on my cell phone. I enter the school's Wi-Fi password (one they don't really give out, but that I've tortured out of Mr. Sanchez. Mathematical torture.) and log in to my blog. Drew was right. The thing has skyrocketed in views since I started blogging about makeup and hair and other crap I don't know anything about.

So, I do the thing that will make or break New York, and, in turn, make or break April's heart: I monetize. After a few minutes, and a post introducing my brilliant scheme, I link it up to PayPal and wait for the questions to fly in.

By lunchtime, one already has. "How to Flirt."

ᚦ

I figure I should give myself a decent amount of time to master this one, so I attempt nothing over the next couple days. "How to Flirt." It's not something I've ever given conscious thought to. And, unfortunately, it's not something I can really enlist Drew's help for. I could show up to his house with unbrushed hair and teeth and last night's mismatched pajamas and he'd still be willing to jump me.

No. This is something I have to inflict on someone . . . potentially more embarrassing. So I walk into cooking with my head held high. The information various Internet sites have given me is all floating around in the back of my mind, and I'm sincerely hoping none of it has been written by some old bald guy who's bored of WoW and has resorted to trolling teens.

"Hey," Seth says when I take my place next to him. Damn, he's hot. I sometimes wonder if he is actually part vampire.

"Hey." *Step One. Make eye contact. For how long? Thirty seconds? Is that too long? Oh my gosh. Stop. Bat your eyelashes. Look away.*

"You okay?" he says, raising his eyebrows.

"Uh, yeah. Just got something in my eye. I think maybe I'm allergic to this class or something."

He laughs. That's a good sign, right?

I head over to the refrigerator to get the pizza dough we made yesterday, and I get Seth's also while I'm there. I drop it on the table in front of him. He's already floured my table for me, which is nice. Ever since a few days ago, with the whole batter-switch/calc-tutoring and then the post-bathroom-weeping incident, we've had this (minimal, I'll admit) alliance.

He unwraps both dough balls while I bend over and reach into the drawer below our station to retrieve a couple rolling pins. And this is where I attempt Flirting Tactic #2: Using Your Assets. I bend over slowly, 'cause these jeans emphasize everything, and then shove my butt out just a little.

Yeah. This is totally working.

Then my butt collides with his legs, and he grunts and two giant lumps of something plop onto my back and then the floor. The dough. I snap upright and whirl around. There's a monstrous smash as my forehead meets his jaw. Blinding pain. BLINDING.

He stumbles backward, rubbing his chin, and I just stand there, clutching my head, beet red, slowly dying.

"Hey, sorry, I, uh, I didn't mean to touch your, um, I'm not like a perv or anything," he says, avoiding my eyes.

He thinks this is *his* fault? Normally, I would say something self-deprecating and take the blame (which really is totally mine). But in this case, well, it's Seth. And it's for science. (Science, a blog, same thing.) So I just shrug and say, "Oh no, it's fine. Don't worry about it."

He scrapes his teeth over his lip and turns back toward the front of the classroom, raising his hand. "Um, Mr. Cole? I dropped our dough. Do you have any extras?"

Mr. Cole makes a disgusted noise and side-eyes me. "*You* dropped them, Mr. Levine?"

"Yeah."

"Perhaps I need to move you farther from Ms. Eisler. It seems she's leeching your powers from you."

I laugh awkwardly and roll both the pins under my hands. Mr. Cole points toward the refrigerator and shakes his head. "Third shelf from the top. I'll have to remove several points from your grade for this, Mr. Levine. Ms. Eisler, yours will remain unchanged."

I can feel the temperature in the room rising, and the beet in my cheeks deepens to crimson. Stupid assets.

Seth slinks over to the fridge and opens the door, then retrieves the balls of dough. He heads back to our table and waits for a second. "Planning on bending over or anything anytime soon?"

"No."

"Good. Then the dough should be safe here." He drops a lump on my table and one on his, then grins at me. I smile back.

Seth unwraps the ball of dough and grabs his rolling pin, then sprinkles the top of the dough with flour. This is something I most definitely would not have done, but I do it anyway, because if Seth does it, it's a safe bet.

Then he starts rolling. I never would have thought that rolling pizza dough could be sexy, but I would have been wrong. His back and shoulders flex as he pushes the pin across the soft ball, flattening and shaping it, and for a minute, I'm so entranced by those muscles I forget to do anything at all to my food.

And then I decide that this is it. Time for Flirting Tactic #3: A Lady's Wit and Charm.

"You know," I say, leaning over to his side of the table and twirling my hair for good measure, "with all the rolling you're doing there you might as well be . . ." *Oh no. I have no idea how to finish this sentence. Don't EVER start a sentence you don't know how to finish.* "Might as well . . . dough . . . roll . . ."

He stops rolling and looks at me, waiting. And . . . nothing. Absolutely nothing.

"I'm, uh. I'm sorry. I think I've just suffered a small stroke."

"Okay," he says, and he goes back to rolling. At that point, I discover that despite my learning, I've been rolling this entire time, and my dough looks like an uneven doughnut. I poke at it for a minute, but nothing I do does anything at all. So I groan and slam my head on my table. Seth jumps.

"You okay?" he asks, setting down his pin beside what I'm sure is the most exquisite pizza crust ever.

"I don't know," I mumble into the flour-coated steel.

"Here," he says. "Let's start this thing over."

I stand up straight, wiping what flour I can from my face, and re-form the pizza-doughnut back into a lump.

"You want to roll like this," he says, gently pushing the rolling pin into the center of the dough, rocking back and forth.

I do the same, or what I think is the same, and within five seconds, the dough is ripping and tearing everywhere.

"Okay, you're close. But it needs to be more like this." And because I've obviously slipped into a parallel universe, Seth reaches in front of me, grabbing my wrists. And then he starts pushing and pulling, forcing my arms to move. He's not behind me or anything; in fact, what he's doing shouldn't be a turn-on, shouldn't be making me dizzy. It's basically nothing but wrist contact. Somehow, though, I can barely focus on the dough. But I have to. I force myself to feel the pressure, the rhythm, everything. And Drew suddenly flashes in front of my face, chest at my back, wrists at my neck, fingers working at that tie. I cough and straighten into Seth, which is no better for my brain. Dammit, Eisler. Pay attention.

I make an attempt.

When Seth steps away, I'm several degrees hotter and my pulse is going crazy, but I'm rolling out a perfect pizza crust.

He gives me a half-cocked grin and goes back to his dough.

Hey, one flirting tactic I can successfully execute: The Damsel in Distress. But I'm not sure how I feel about that.

7. How to Give Yourself a Bikini Wax (or Die Trying)

I rap twice on April's front door, not because I have to, but because once, when I decided to take advantage of my "You don't have to knock; you're family" status, I walked in on April's dad in his underwear. He's not the kind of dad you want to see in his underwear. And who does that, anyway? Either way, I've knocked ever since. April has not questioned my decision.

She yells what sounds like "Come in," but could honestly be just about anything. Her front door is solid wood and not optimal for sound wave travel. I give it a couple seconds, lest I misheard, and open the door. I breathe a sigh of relief when I see her dad, fully clothed, sitting on the couch. He waves and smiles, and I wave back.

"Renley? Sweetie?" her mom calls from the kitchen. She comes out in an apron, apricot heels, and red lipstick. I swear one day she was just beamed here from 1943. Which is basically adorable.

"Hey," I say back.

"Do you want some cookies? They're oatmeal raisin." Of course they are. I'm surprised there's no homemade apple pie cooling on the windowsill. (Maybe there is.)

"I'm good, but thanks!" I say, bounding up the stairs to April's room. The door is already open, so I just flit in and drop my bag onto her already-cluttered floor.

"Don't try the cookies," she says. "They're Satan. Oatmeal-raisin Satan cookies."

"That can't be good."

"Mom is into this gluten-free living shit she found online somewhere. And like, coconut flour instead of sugar or something? I don't know. What I do know is that they have come from hell to destroy us; do not give in."

I snort and she sits up, brushing her bangs out of her face. "So. We're highlighting your hair. Bleach blonde?"

"Yes." I pull out a cheap thing of dye from the drugstore and toss it over to her. She inspects it, turning it over several times, like she's a professional stylist.

"I'm borrowing some of this," she says. "You're putting blue in my hair."

"And you're bleaching it?"

She rolls her eyes. "You know nothing of fashiony ways, Padawan. You can't just dye black hair blue. You have to strip the color out first."

I nod, mentally filing that away for a blog post later. I still haven't written the dreaded flirting advice, because let's face it, that attempt was the worst thing anyone has ever tried to do. But I've had a couple of other requests come through. At the moment, my focus is highlighting hair at home, as well as something . . . more painful.

"Okay, I also bought this." I throw a box at her and hide my face.

"This is—this is a bikini waxing kit."

"I'm aware."

"You want me to help you wax your vagina?"

I steal a small cover from her bed and hide my face in it. "Oh my gosh." I peek out from the cover to see her eyes shoot wide open.

"Is this because you're gonna *show it* to someone?"

"No!" I shout, and I fling myself back on her bed. I'm immediately consumed by pillows. She has so many pillows of ridiculous shapes and sizes, most of the time, you can't even see her bed.

She cackles when my face turns the color of a blood orange and rips open the package. I snatch it back from her. "We are *not* doing this first. Get the bleach, you sadist."

She's still cackling when she opens the package of dye and pulls out the flimsy plastic gloves that come with the kit.

"Hold on a sec," I say. "I need to go wash my hair."

"No!" she yells, and I jump. "You don't wash before you bleach. You have to leave it gross and oily, or it'll get all screwed up and fry your hair."

I stay seated between a giant frog and even more giant Tootsie Roll pillow, fiddling with the fabric at the end of it. I'm starting to question if this tutorial was totally worth it, but I only need five people to pay for the answer to break even—and a few more if I manage to screw this up royally and need to pay for therapy.

"Okay," April says, steepling her fingers and grinning psychotically, "get in ze chair."

I get up slowly and slink over, like someone walking the green mile.

"Do not fear, my child. Zis will be painless." She laughs maniacally again, throwing her head back. I am not reassured.

I snatch the box from the vanity and dump out the contents.

"I need a bowl to mix this stuff in."

She prances out of the room and down to the kitchen, and I rifle through the supplies. This could be, well, a disaster. Really, this whole thing could fail, and I'd be stuck here and not in New York, and then April would shrivel and die. That would be the worst-case scenario.

I only have seven months left to get three grand, and so far I've made . . . twenty bucks. I'm pretty sure some of that is because Drew pays for answers to everything I post. But even so, I know I have a few other followers out there. I mean, I have more than a few now. Just not many who've been enticed into paying for answers. Which is why I have to go full-throttle. Capitalize on the few now. And no one ever got anything worth having without taking a risk, right? (In this case, those risks being my hair and my bikini line.)

April returns with a small mixing bowl and I pour in the solution and stir it around, then let it sit. I lean back in the chair and spin it slowly while we wait. April flips on her docking station and something loud blares through the speakers. Something punk I don't recognize.

Within thirty seconds, an even louder country song blasts through the walls. April's eyes narrow and she pushes the door open. Keith casually walks out of the room next door and grins at her.

"What are you doing?" she asks. More like *accuses*, but you can't really accuse a question.

"Listening to music."

"Well stop playing that crap so loud right next to me."

"*This* is crap? I don't even know what to call whatever's coming through your speakers."

"Just turn it down," she says, a sigh in her voice.

"Turn yours down." He laughs when she just stands there, arms crossed. "Well, whatever. I'm going downstairs to get a Satan-cookie."

He turns his back and starts down the stairs and April turns just a fraction toward his door.

"*Don't* go in my room while I'm gone. There will be consequences," he calls from the stairwell.

"UGGGHHH, KEITH. I HATE YOU SO MUCH," she yells. She won't go in there. Keith's justice is swift and merciless, and not worth a country music reprieve. She rolls her eyes and sighs about as loudly as anyone is capable of sighing but then she runs back over to the bannister and yells, "I'm just kidding; I love you, please don't leave for college next year and never come back!"

Keith took a few years off after graduation to pursue a career in comic book art. That hasn't exactly panned out yet, so I guess his parents are pressuring him to figure something out. College, maybe? Which makes me laugh. I just can't think of Keith as a college man.

I hear his resonant laugh from all the way downstairs. Sometimes, when I see Keith and April, I wonder what it would be like to have a sibling. But she hates him half the time, so maybe it wouldn't be so awesome.

April sits back on her pillow-bed and stares venomously at the docking station. After minutes of deliberating, she finally rolls her eyes at nothing and turns the thing off. Seconds later, the country music comes to a mysterious end as well. She makes an exasperated huff-noise.

"This dye should be pretty much done now."

"Oh. Yeah." The annoyance is still swimming across her face, but it's somewhat dulled. In two minutes she will have forgotten it completely.

She grabs some clips and pins up my hair in haphazard lumps. The foil crinkles in my ear as she lays it around my hair. I start shaking my leg. The closer she gets to applying the bleach, the more nervous I am.

"Relax," she says. "I've done this ten thousand times. You think my hair naturally changes colors every couple months?"

That reminder does relax me a little. After several minutes, the bleach is applied and my head is so foily, I'm pretty sure I can pick up the local radio station.

"Now me." April whips the chair around and flings me out of it. I am glad, for once, for the mountain of pillows separating the mattress and me, and land in a giant cloud of fat, stuffed things. She sits and hands me the bleach. I just sit there, holding the brush and the bleach, not blinking. She should not trust me with this.

"Stop being a wuss. Just paint it here"—she gestures to the tips of her blunt bangs—"and then down here"—she moves her fingers in stripes down from her bangs to the ends of her hair at her shoulders—"and then connect them together at the back." She spins around and moves both her fingers across the bottom back edge of her hair, until they meet in the middle.

"So, you want, like, a bleach outline of your hair. Like, if someone took a Sharpie and drew around it, or you were a cartoon or something."

"Yes. But it's not gonna be bleach forever. After, I'm dying it aqua blue. Look at it!"

She rummages through the top drawer of her vanity and pulls out a dented box, then throws it at me. It is extremely aqua blue. Which, to me, just seems bizarre. And on me, that's how it would look. Probably on April, though, it will look like punk-rock Barbie.

I take a deep breath and start to paint.

"What if I kill your hair?"

"Hair is already dead. So you can't possibly kill it. Plus, I put a crap ton of olive oil in it last night and again before you came over. So my hair will be fry-free and beautiful."

Olive oil hair. Gross. But also, store that away for the blog.

I dutifully continue to outline her hair and foil it. By the end, she looks a little like a character from an eighties cyberpunk movie.

"So," she says, "while we wait for that to work, we might as well wax your vag."

"Ugh, forget I said anything about it. This is stupid and ridiculous."

"Fine, but you brought it up."

I sit on her bed, fiddling with various fluffy things, then look up at her.

"So, Keith's going to college next fall? I thought he wanted to be a Marine or something."

Her face falls immediately, and I wish I hadn't said anything.

"I don't even know right now. He was all set to be, like, an accountant. Then, he met this stupid recruiter and freaking rocked his ASVAB and now he can't stop talking about it."

I'm not sure exactly how to respond. "Well, I mean, it's a noble thing."

"Yeah, I know. It's noble and honorable and great. I just don't want Keith to do it. I don't want him to get . . ." She looks at nothing, over my shoulder.

"I—" I start. But she puts on a giant, plastic smile and bounces up.

"I saw Cash again last night."

So that's the end of that conversation.

"How'd it go?"

She grins. "Let's just say, guys love making out with a girl with a lip ring."

I have no idea how it would make much of a difference; it's in her upper lip. But, sure. I smile. "Lucky."

"Are you *still* not making out with your super-hot neighbor?"

"No," I say firmly.

"I don't get that. At. All. If I had a neighbor like that who worshipped the ground I walked on, I'd be over there all the time."

"I *am* over there all the time."

She rolls her eyes. "Yes, exactly. You're over there all the time, cuddling, sleeping in his *bed*, and who knows what else, and you're not even making out?"

I start playing with my hands. "It's complicated."

"Not from where I'm sitting."

And, because we're hitting on a topic that I am not excited to talk about or think about, I change the subject with the only thing I know will do it: "Okay, let's wax this."

She laughs and opens the kit. "What do you want? A landing strip? A heart? Or ooooh! A star!"

There are seriously *stencils* for this? I immediately regret my decision and back away.

"Oh come on," she says, seeing me inch backward. "It doesn't even hurt."

I raise an eyebrow. "It doesn't?"

"No. It comes with this numbing stuff that works super well. It's like plucking your eyebrows."

I screw up my mouth and eye her. "Then why don't you do it with me?"

"Because I did it two weeks ago."

"Oh."

She starts to heat the wax strips in her hands. I decide not to go with a stencil. I don't want to look like a stripper. I shouldn't do this. It isn't worth the money. But yes, yes it is. Because April will die if I don't go to New York with her. And really, it's not just about her. Now that I've basically already experienced the sting of my mom rejecting me, I want to go. I would kill to go.

She hands me the numbing stuff. "Okay, woman. Get naked."

I hop over to the other side of the bed, just out of her line of sight, and half strip. Then I apply the numbing stuff. This better work. She hands me the strips.

"Um . . . are you . . ." my heartbeat is in my throat. I can feel it. Major pain is coming, I know it. "Are you sure this isn't going to hurt?"

"Positive. I seriously *just* did this. It's not bad at all."

I let out a somewhat relieved sigh and take the strips from her.

"Put them where you want them," she commands.

I take a deep breath and stick.

"Wait a minute. You want the wax to totally adhere."

Oh man, I'm gonna die. But there's nothing I can do now.

"On the count of three. Take two of them. And when I say three, pull."

I am about to hyperventilate. I know it's ridiculous. April said it wouldn't even hurt. She said—

"One . . ."

I roll my shoulders and crack my neck, like I'm prepping for a boxing match.

"Two . . ."

And grab the strips.

"Three."

Pull.

I scream.

"April, you slut-whore lady douchebag!" I am in so much pain I can't even think of more awful things to call her. She actually falls out of her chair, she's laughing so hard.

"Why?" I gasp, between bouts of tearing up. "Why would you tell me that? This is worse than CHILDBIRTH."

She can't even breathe, she's laughing so hard. But between her chortles, she manages, "Get the others out! You can't just walk around with wax strips stuck to your lady bits!"

I can. Yes, I can. I look down. No, I freaking can't. So, I rip out the other four. Quick and painful. "Seriously, April, you just did this two weeks ago? There's no way you forgot this level of pain."

"No, dude. I did one strip and it hurt so bad I just cut the rest out." And then she's giggling that evil witch giggle again.

I have never hated someone so much in my life. I hope she dies of laughter-induced oxygen deprivation. If she did, I wouldn't even take the foil out of her hair. She could just go to the afterlife looking like a cyborg. I don't even care.

I collapse onto the floor, clutching everything, and fuming and trying not to cry, because that's stupid. And then she says, "Oh! Time to take out your bleach!"

I don't want her near my hair. But also, I do. So I lie there for another minute or two and get up. "Fine. Do it. I'm not touching yours."

She laughs again and takes the foil out. Then I head to the shower. I'm not in there long, just long enough to rinse out the bleach and attempt to soothe my on-fire vag. But by the time I get out, I'm ready to at least look at April. Honestly, I'm charging more for this answer than any of the others so far, so her douchebaggery was kind of helpful. Still.

I avoid looking too pleased while she dries my hair. She has me spun around so I can't see myself in the mirror. Then, she smiles, obviously impressed with herself. "Alright, my newly groomed friend. No more moping. Look."

She spins me around and my jaw drops. I look . . . amazing.

8. How to Be Awesome

I spend the rest of the weekend holed up in my room, which is a bit of a shame, considering the new perfect hair. But it just makes the following Monday that much more awesome.

I head out the door and over to Drew's, running a hand through my hair and fluffing it a little for good measure. I knock, only because I'm about ten minutes early. After a few seconds, he opens the door and just stands there. His gaze travels from the top of my head down to my toes and lingers at several key places on the way back up. Normally, I would feel self-conscious, but wearing what I'm wearing, looking how I look, I just . . . don't.

"Wow," he says.

I suddenly start to feel a little embarrassed and look away. "Thanks," I say, smoothing down my fitted red top over my jeans, which feel just a tad too tight.

"Taking your own advice, I see."

I laugh. "Well, trying to. I am nothing if not authentic. And you know, certified expert and all."

"Highlighted hair, jeans that show off 'your best assets,'"—his voice goes super high when he says this, mimicking mine—"a bikini wax?" He raises an eyebrow and grins. My face goes instantly hot; I know it's probably redder than my shirt. Sometimes I forget Drew reads everything I post.

"Don't even get me started on that."

He snickers. "Give me just a couple minutes, okay? I need to grab a jacket and, you know, put on shoes."

"Fair enough."

I step inside and lean against the doorframe, feeling weird. Like, I don't know. Someone else. But at this exact moment, it feels kind of good. And that's okay, I think.

A small person I don't recognize pads past me and adjusts the thick glasses on the top of her nose. She's got to be at least nineteen, and the college hoodie tells me my instincts are not wrong. She stiffens when she sees me and narrows her eyes, looking me up and down in the exact same places Drew did, but in a very different way.

"Hi," I say.

She lets out an exasperated sigh, clutching a small backpack to her chest, and pushes past me and out the door. Drew meets me about two minutes later, raking a hand through his hair and grinning sheepishly. I click my tongue.

"Keeping her up late on a school night? You knave."

He shrugs and slings a bag over his shoulder, simultaneously pushing the front door open. "Eh, her first class isn't until ten today. She'll live. And she'll think it was worth it."

He winks at me and I roll my eyes. Then, as we walk across the yard and to his car (cold front decided to swoop in this week and usher out October), I frown. I slip into the front seat, trying not to look weird when he hops in and fastens his seatbelt.

"Did she . . . she stayed over?"

"Yeah," he says, and he spends at least thirty seconds attempting to start the ignition.

I blink and look out the window, not knowing what to do with the hot flash of jealousy that floods over me. This is stupid. And totally not fair. I'm not allowed to be jealous, and usually I'm not, because Drew and I are nothing that allows me to be possessive. He sleeps with girls all the time, but . . . some cougar college girl shouldn't be sleeping over at Drew's. Only I'm allowed to do that.

"Why?" he asks after the silence has gone on just long enough to be awkward. "Are you jealous?" He's teasing; I can hear it in his voice. But I can't look directly at him, and it's so stupid.

Out of the corner of my eye, I see the smile on his face disappear, and his eyebrows rise. Then he furrows his brow and turns back to face the road.

"Uh, it's not like I asked her to stay over or anything. You know how I feel about that. It's just, I don't know, I think she expected to stay or something. I don't know how this all works with college girls." He glances at me, hands twisting on the wheel. "It felt really weird waking up with her next to me."

Now I feel even more like an idiot. And a jerk. Why is he apologizing to me? What did he do? Cheat on his not-girlfriend, not even friend-with-benefits? But I can't make myself look or feel like a reasonable human being. All I can do is stutter.

"No it's um, it's totally fine. It's uh . . . it's not like . . . um . . ." Eloquent.

"She was a one-time thing. She's not my girlfriend or something, just because she spent the night at my house."

"It doesn't matter." I swallow hard, trying to take the crazy jealous rasp out of my voice. "Even if she was, why would I care about that? Date whoever you want."

He does this terse headshake thing and clenches his jaw, staring, unblinking, at the road. What was I supposed to say? *Don't date anyone but me, even though you can't date me?* He can't really be pissed about that.

I wish now that it was still warm enough to run to school. Then maybe this whole super awkward exchange would have been avoided. As it is, there are still a couple minutes left until we get to school, and the car is very suddenly suffocating. I lean my head against the window, wondering exactly when things got complicated between Drew and me. When exactly it happened that there were certain things we couldn't talk about. When I'd decided that all my ridiculous abandonment issues were something I could attach to him. And when I had decided it was my right to be jealous, not because he slept with another girl, but because he hadn't kicked her out of bed five minutes after. When, in my warped subconscious, had his bed become mine?

The silence is so uncomfortable that I know we can both feel it on our skin. Drew clears his throat and steals a glance at me. "So. You, uh, check your blog lately?"

The quick switch of subject is jarring, but welcome, and the relief is clear on his face when I grab hold of the change.

"Of course."

"You're getting pretty popular already, right? From the amount of questions you've been answering. And I've heard people talking about it in the hallways."

A huge smile spreads across my face. "Really? People are talking about me? It hasn't even been that long."

"Yeah, sometimes. You must be making some actual money."

I shrug. "I don't know; I haven't actually checked that in like a week."

He furrows his brow. I guess it *is* a little weird, being that New York is why I started this thing in the first place. But whatever.

The car grinds to a halt as we reach the parking lot, and another silence, somehow even more awkward than the first one, pops up. I am *so* glad this ride is over. I step out of the car and shut the door behind me, making my way to the front door.

"Hey, R, I, um, have a couple things going on after school today. Can you get another ride home?"

He's lying. But I don't blame him. I don't want to suffer through another ride with him either. "Yeah, no problem."

Before I can say anything else, April comes running out the front doors and grabs me by the arm. "You! Are so sexy I thought maybe I was bi for, like, five seconds."

I laugh and steal one last glimpse over at Drew, feeling like, somehow, the whole dumb argument (or whatever it was) should be resolved already. He just gives me a half wave. And we go our separate ways.

☗

I'm probably imagining the looks in the hallways, and I'm certainly imagining the theme music and wind in my hair as I strut down the hall. Strut, strut, strut. Drew can suck it.

Seth waves at me as I enter cooking and I wave back and smile. Look at me, all not awkward and butt-bumping him all over the place. I take my seat next to him and he turns back to a crumpled paper, massacred with an eraser worn down to the metal. He chews on the end of his pencil, frowning so hard I think the lines from that single expression might be permanent.

It's weird seeing him like this. "You okay?" I ask.

He grunts in response.

"Um . . . need help?"

He slams the pencil down and rubs his forehead, then shakes his head and stares at me with the most adorable puppy dog eyes I've ever seen, including those of real puppies.

"Trigonometry, man. It's the devil. I never thought I would bear so much ill will toward a shape."

I nod, like I can relate, even though I can't. Trig always came as easily to me as breathing. But still.

"I'm going to fail this class. I'm gonna fail it, wreck my GPA, kill my chances at a scholarship . . ." He groans and lets his head fall with alarming momentum to his table. It thuds and just rests there.

I sigh and grab the paper from under his cheek. It takes me about five seconds to find the error he's making.

"I see what you're doing here. You just—"

The bell rings and Mr. Cole clears his throat loudly, taking his place at the head of the class.

Seth takes a sidelong look at me and pulls a fresh sheet of paper out of his bag. He scrawls something on it, then passes it over to me.

I can barely read it—boy handwriting is like a different language. But after several laborious minutes, I make out:

do you do any tutoring?

No. But I would *happily* tutor Seth.

Sure.

He looks at my note and smiles.

how much $?

I'll trade you for cooking lessons.

He snickers and reaches across the table to shake my hand. Very official. I take his hand and try to ignore the wave of tingles that travels up my arm. *He has a girlfriend. He has a girlfriend.*

How about today after school? I write.

He nods and folds up the note, then sticks it in his back pocket. Then we both look forward and pretend to pay attention to Mr. Cole.

Ride home acquired.

9. HOW to Get a Not-Date With the Hottest Guy in School

When cooking ends, Seth follows me out of class.

"Do you have a car?" he asks.

I give him a falsely solemn look and shrug. "Sophomore. I mean, I have a license. But no car."

"Ah, the trials of the young." He takes out a set of keys from his pocket and twirls it around his finger, smirking.

"Alas, we underclassmen truly are a pitiful breed. It's why we keep you seniors around." I lean back against the wall and smile, crossing my arms over my chest.

He narrows his eyes. "Our cars? Now, that can't be the *only* reason." That half grin is still on his face when he leans over me, hand pressed just an inch or two above my shoulder. My heart starts going crazy. Is this . . . are we flirting? I think . . . there's no way.

I blink at him, suddenly forgetting what we were talking about in the first place. He looks at my clearly confused-but-thrilled eyes and blinks himself, then glances over at his own bicep, like he hasn't realized he was doing "the lean." Then he straightens and looks around, clearing his throat.

"Anyway, yeah. So, you want to just hitch a ride to my house then?"

He's avoiding looking straight at my eyes, which confirms (unbelievably) that we were totally flirting.

"Sure," I say. "I'll just meet you out front. What kind of car do you drive?"

"A black Lexus."

I raise an eyebrow, somewhat impressed.

"I know, it's lame. But I got it from my dad and . . . anyway, I have a couple quick things to take care of, but I can meet you in the parking lot in ten. Cool?"

"Cool."

Over his shoulder, I can see his girlfriend heading toward us. She slows and smiles brightly at me, and I feel this overwhelming flash of guilt, like discussing tutoring was something really wrong. Taylor is one of those popular people who is popular for a reason; she's kind of unhateable.

"Hi," she says, giant smile still plastered on her face.

Seth wraps his arm around her waist and nods at me. "Hey, Tay. This is—"

"Renley Eisler. I know. Cute hair."

"Thanks," I choke out, wondering when exactly Taylor Krissick learned of my existence.

She waves this little Miss America wave and spins around, practically pulling Seth behind her. I'm not sure how that's possible, since he's the one with his arm around her, but she's very clearly leading their descent down the hall. I see her perfect pink expression darken the second they swivel, and Seth stiffens, looking in the other direction. Interesting.

And as soon as they're out of my line of sight, I text April everything. She responds with nothing but a winky face. Of course she does.

I walk out the front door, following the sea of bodies into the courtyard, then break off from the crowd, going to sit against the red brick of the school building, inhaling that grass-just-before-fall smell. I stick a headphone in my ear and halfway listen to something kind of lame and mainstream that I secretly adore, and I watch. I've got nothing else to do for the next ten—more like eight—minutes.

Across the way, I see Drew walking down the sidewalk, fists shoved in his pockets, looking sad. Or mad. It's impossible to tell with him most of the time. And, just like I thought this morning, he does a 90-degree turn and heads straight for his car in the front of the lot. Something going on after school. Freaking liar. I stare daggers at the back of his head, almost hoping he'll turn around. But then he does, and I'm embarrassed that he saw me looking at him like one of us was the spawn of Satan. (I'm not sure which one, in this scenario.)

He scrapes his lower lip with his teeth and then shakes his head, turning around and sticking a key in his car door, jiggling it.

I roll my eyes and look the other way, waiting for my hotter ride with a sexier car to show up. Eventually, he and America's Next Top Model emerge from the school, his arm still glued to her waist. He gets to his car, and I don't get up. Taylor backs up just slightly, freeing herself from his arm, and she looks . . . pissed. She starts gesturing in a giant but controlled way, like those whisper-yells you do sometimes to imitate a scream when people are watching. Seth doesn't even react. He just stands there, arms crossed, leaning against the Lexus, saying nothing. Eventually, she throws her hands in the air and bows her head a little, then leans up on her tiptoes to kiss him. He looks the other way, so her lips just barely brush his jaw, and she stomps off in her high heels. That much force on that small a surface area looks extremely painful.

When he gets in his car and starts the engine, it doesn't scream like Drew's car, which is a welcome change of pace. I get up and walk slowly toward the pick-up area, slinging my backpack over my shoulder. He waves when he sees me approach and leans over and pops the door open. I get inside and click my seatbelt into place, throwing my backpack over into the backseat.

"What are you listening to?" Seth asks.

"Oh." I'm immediately embarrassed by my less-than-hipster music choice. "Nothing, it's just something stupid."

"Hey, no judgment here. You listen to your pop rap dance-house stuff, whatever."

I grin and take the headphone out of my ear, then take a look around his car. It's clean, super clean. And it smells like strawberries and sugar. I bet there's a girly air freshener stowed somewhere in here.

"What are you looking for?"

"The scent thing you definitely got from Bath and Body Works. It's somewhere around here." I pop open his glove box, then realize afterward just what an invasion of privacy that is.

"Dude, are you snooping in my car while I'm *right here*?"

I know my face is like a cherry—it's one of the things I hate most about myself. Anything somewhat embarrassing, and bam. Bright red. And probably sweaty.

He laughs, which lessens the cherry-red to a kind of bubblegum pink; I can feel the shade change in the heat on my cheeks.

"You are an interesting person," he says, still chuckling.

"Fair enough."

"The candy smell thing was from Taylor, by the way. And I'm pretty sure it's called Visions of Sugarplums. She's, uh, my girlfriend."

"Yeah, I gathered that," I say, crossing my arms instinctively, trying not to appear jealous.

He glances over at me, then back at the road, and I see a tiny smile playing at the corner of his mouth. He definitely noticed.

"We've been together for six months now. I mean, this time."

"Oh." I don't really know what else to say to that.

"And you, you're with that kid Drew, right?"

I shake my head. "Seriously? Drew?"

"I thought you guys were a thing."

I let out an exasperated laugh. "Yeah, no. Drew and I have *never* been a thing. Not with all the girls he screws on a nightly basis. No, thank you."

"Well, that was . . . blunt. So no you-and-Drew then."

"No."

And that little smile again that makes my insides flutter. Dumb. He just said he and Taylor had been together for half a year, which is a long time. Even if there does seem to be a little trouble in paradise, that's no reason to be jumping for joy. They've broken up and gotten back together a thousand times since middle school. They're the golden couple, and the golden couple stays together till they graduate, then they get married and have beautiful golden babies.

"And you and Taylor. You guys . . ." I trail off when I see his shoulders sag at the mention of her name. "Okay, never mind."

"It's nothing," he says. "It's just that lately, we—what am I saying? You don't care about my relationship problems; I barely know you."

That stings, even though it's true. I stare out the window, somewhat disenchanted with the ride-tutor situation now that Taylor has been brought to the forefront of both our minds. But at least I'm not the only one she seems to have doused with a bucket of cold water. I shouldn't be pleased that Seth isn't thrilled with his relationship, but whatever. I am.

Seth turns to the right and I straighten when he enters a neighborhood I've only ever driven by and lusted after.

It's not full of McMansions or anything, but the houses are nice. Way nice. Way nicer than any of my friends' houses.

He stops in front of a stucco one with a stamped concrete driveway and a perfectly manicured lawn. I get out of the car and smooth my hair and shirt, feeling totally out of place, like I need to de-wrinkle to fit with the picture before I step in.

He doesn't seem to notice my unease and walks ahead of me to his front door. He pushes it open and holds it for me, which is nice, and I try not to stare when I head toward the entry.

There's a little silver thing hanging on the right side of the doorway at an angle. I cock my head and glance at it.

"Mezuzah," he says. "Not a poorly installed doorbell."

"Oh. Yeah. Of course," I say. I was, in fact, thinking extremely fancy doorbell for tall people.

We step farther inside and he says, "One sec, Renley, I just need to tell my parents you're here, so they're not pissed."

He walks through the tiled entryway down a corridor, then disappears. I whip out my phone and type.

April, I'm in Seth Levine's living room.

Ooooooh. Have you gone into his BEDROOM yet? ;) ;) ;)

You are such a slut.

I'm not the one in Seth Levine's bedroom.

I roll my eyes. I write, **NEITHER AM I.**

She sends back a bunch more winky faces and a couple obscene emojis that really should never have been invented. I slide the phone quickly into my pocket as Seth walks back in.

"Do you want something to drink?"

"Would you happen to have Dr Pepper?"

He takes two out of the fridge and acts like he's going to throw mine to me. This is a move he will regret, because I *will* dodge something heavy flying at me, even if I could feasibly catch it.

"Kidding," he says, and he takes a seat at the table. "I make a point of not hurling projectile sodas at girls when they come over."

I don't know why a little thrill courses through me when he says that. I am a girl. I am over. Maybe it has something to do with him calling me a girl, not, like, a tutor. 'Cause he sees me as a girl, which, coming back full circle here, is what I am, so who gives a crap?

I sit in the chair next to his and pop open the soda, then take a drink. Sweet, almost burning. I will never get over my love of Dr Pepper. Ever. He takes a drink from his, too, and looks at me expectantly.

"So . . . do you have your trig book?"

He blinks. "Oh yeah. Tutoring. Duh. One sec." Then he runs out the door. Presumably, he left his backpack in his car. Did he actually forget that was why I was here?

He comes back in, looking sheepish, then sits down next to me. He drops his bag on the floor next to him and procures his massive trigonometry book, his notebook, and his abused homework.

"I just need to warn you, I suck at this. Hardcore."

I don't even think before I say, "Well, it wouldn't be fair if you were good at it. There's a rule against being hot, a cooking extraordinaire, *and* a math whiz. Not fair to the other guys."

He grins widely, mischievously, but then drops his gaze from my face, twirling the chain around his neck nervously. A chain I'm sure, suddenly, is from Taylor. Stupid. But the grin never goes away, even when we're discussing the thing he hates most in the world. And that has got to be a good sign.

NOVEMBER

10. HOW to GO parking With a Guy

I've been running to school the past several days. It's dumb, because it's really starting to get cold outside, and I know that if I showed up to Drew's house, he would give me a ride. And I could always just take the bus, but, honestly, I live super close to school—close enough I hardly break a sweat—and I'd rather run in the cold than deal with the bus.

After like four days of this, though, it's starting to get old, and I can't even remember what exactly we were even fighting about. I know it had something to do with a college girl.

I glance out the window and see that there's no light on in Drew's room. It's after ten so that could mean he's sleeping or getting laid or doing nothing. I take a chance, and pull my cell out of my jeans, then scroll through the messages one last time, just to be sure I haven't missed any from him. I haven't. That kind of pisses me off, so the text I send him may not come off as sugar sweet.

I need to talk to you.

He doesn't respond for a few minutes, but I get dressed anyway, pulling a light sweater over my head and running a brush through my hair. Then the phone vibrates.

Come over.

I pad down the stairs in my socks, but freeze at the door when I hear, "Leelee?"

"Yeah?"

My dad is sitting at the kitchen table in a robe, eating a bowl of cereal. He pushes his glasses up his nose and stares at me, then at the clock. "Where you going?"

I shrug. "Drew's."

He stares down at his cereal and scratches his head awkwardly. His voice is quieter when he speaks next. "It's ten-thirty at night, honey."

I glance at the clock. "Yup."

"Do you think . . . do you think going to a boy's house after dark, especially a boy like *that*, is great judgment on your part?"

I roll my eyes. "Dad, come on. Are we going to pretend now that I don't go over there every night after ten-thirty?"

He shifts back in his seat and stares up at me, fiddling with the spoon between his fingers.

"Leelee, I'm not happy about this. I don't want to say you can't go, but—"

"Okay, then. Good talk." I turn around to face the door.

He slams his spoon down and milk sloshes over the side of his bowl. "Are you not even giving me the courtesy of lying anymore when you sneak out to go screw someone?"

I blink several times. I've never heard my dad talk like this, but the shock wears off about as quickly as it came, and I lower my voice. "I learned from the best, Dad."

He drops his spoon and his mouth hangs open. He doesn't even blink for several seconds. I open the door and shut it quietly behind me. He doesn't follow, not that that's surprising. And when I'm outside in the cold dark, I run my hands over my eyes and wipe away the few tears burning at the corners of them.

Drew is waiting on the front porch of his house, and I'm glad for the dark. Not that I'm embarrassed to cry in front of him, but I don't want to talk about this right now. Maybe ever. To anyone. I'd rather just be pissed off at Drew and talk about that.

He stands when he sees me coming toward him and makes like he's going to give me a hug, something else I don't want right now. I stop just short of his arms and he drops them.

"Keys?"

"What?" he says, visibly annoyed.

"Do you have the keys? To your car?"

"Yeah, sure. You need them?"

"I want to go somewhere."

"It's cold out."

"Not that cold," I say, and he tosses me the keys. "Come on, wuss."

He hesitates on his porch for a minute, then sighs loudly and follows me to his car.

I hop in the driver's seat and he slowly gets in to the passenger's. Once he clicks his seatbelt into place, I start (or attempt to start) the engine. It takes me several tries.

"You have to hold down the—"

"I know. I've driven a stick before," I snap. He leans back in his seat and stares straight ahead. I don't even know why I'm so pissed now. I thought I came over because I missed him.

Once I finally get the car to start and we're rattling down the road, he rolls his head over to look at me. "So, did you text me just to yell and be mad at me all night? Cause I'd rather just go home if that's your plan."

I don't answer. I don't even know.

"Where are we going anyway?" he asks.

"Where do you think?"

He laughs, but it's devoid of the humor one usually expects from a laugh. "Oh great. Alone in the woods at night with a pissed off woman. Please don't murder me."

This actually does make me smile. "It's not really the woods. Not deep in them, anyway."

Drew's radio doesn't work, and neither of us feels like talking yet, so the rest of the drive is pretty quiet. Luckily, it's a spot just a few minutes outside of town.

The car sputters to a halt and we both just sit there for a couple minutes, neither of us saying anything. We've never really fought—over anything—so this feels strange. Threatening. Like we'll get out of the car and talk about everything, and then the whole relationship will change. Break.

He looks over at me once the silence has thickened and pops the headlights on so we can see, pushes open his door, then closes it behind him. I have no choice but to follow.

"It's cold," I say, hugging the light sweater around my body, wishing I'd brought something heavier.

"I told you," he replies. Then he opens up his back door and rummages through the backseat for something. It doesn't take long; he likes to keep his backseat empty, for obvious reasons.

He emerges with a blanket and hands it to me.

"Not gonna offer me your jacket?" I ask him, teasing.

"I don't see why I should freeze just 'cause you didn't think to bring a coat." He smiles, teasing back, and tosses me the blanket. I immediately start to relax. This feels normal.

"So you're giving me a blanket instead. Trying to seduce me, obviously."

"Obviously."

He climbs up on the hood of his car and reaches down to help me up. The hood pops and settles beneath our weight, but it's so dented and we've done this so many times by now, he doesn't care.

I wrap the blanket around me. It's fuzzy and smells clean, which is a relief.

"Hey," I say, a small laugh in my voice, "you remember when we were little kids and we tried to cross the creek behind our yards?"

He laughs. "On that little log? We were what, like, five and six? How do you even remember that?"

"My mom freaked out and tried to help us cross and you got pissed and then we all ended up falling in that briar patch across the creek," I say.

"Didn't you end up going to the hospital?"

"Six stitches," I say, and I roll up my pant leg. "Still have a scar."

He reaches across me to the little white line on my calf and runs his thumb across it.

"When did everything change?" I whisper, and he doesn't answer.

He takes a deep breath and exhales, and we both stall for a little while again, staring out over the city. From here, you can see it all. Twinkling lights like little stars that have fallen from the sky. Trees behind, the city ahead. It's the perfect spot—away from school, the house, Dad . . . the perfect spot.

I wonder fleetingly how many girls Drew has deflowered here. That brings everything back to the present.

"How many . . ." I stop, feeling strange.

He looks at me. "How many what?"

"How many other girls have you brought here? Besides me?"

"Now that you mention it, this *would* be the ideal place. It's totally romantic." He's being playful, which is normal, but I'm just not in the mood. He senses it immediately and the glint in his eye disappears. "None. No one's been here with me but you. This is our spot."

That makes me feel good, then guilty for feeling good about it.

Drew lies back on the hood of the car, arm open, and I lie back with him, head nestled in the crook of his arm. I can feel his pulse speeding. We are not five and six anymore, and our biggest issues do not revolve around briar patches in a creek. So whatever it is that he wants to say is stressing him out.

"Just say it, Drew."

He breathes deeply in and out several times. Then, "You know, it's not really fair of you."

I go hot everywhere. "What's not fair?"

"You know I'd be with you in a second. You say the word, and I'm in, completely. But *I* know you don't want that. You've made it perfectly clear. And that's fine. And I'm not gonna say, 'Quit leading me on,' because I know that when you stay over at my house and lay your head on my chest, you're not saying you want to be with me." He shifts, and I can feel the sudden tension in his arm, the light quickening of his pulse. I'm sure mine rises to the occasion. His fingers tighten nervously on my shoulder and he takes a deep breath. "But I call bullshit on you getting pissed off at who I sleep with."

I just lie there, face going from hot to on fire. "I know. And I don't even, I don't even know why I got so crazy over that. But that's not why I'm mad at you, anyway. You didn't even talk to me for four days. Not a text."

He looks over at me and narrows his eyes, then back up at the sparkling sky. He's not going to let the change of subject go completely, but he plays along. "You're right. I was kind of a dick about the whole thing. I'll go with that. I should have texted or called you."

"Yeah." I'm shaking everywhere. He runs his fingers up and down my arm, probably trying to calm me even though he's pissed. I hate confrontation more than anything, especially when it seems pretty clear that I'm wrong.

"But my phone wasn't exactly buzzing all week either," he says.

I have nothing to say to that. So I don't.

"And you're not getting out of everything that easy. I'm mad at you, R."

"You are?"

I roll away from him when he props himself up on an elbow and looks down at me. "Yeah. I am. You don't get to decide who I can and can't make out with, or sleep with, or do *anything* I want with. Because we're not together. And I'm not going to worry about your feelings every time I invite a girl over, because you have no idea what those feelings even are."

"And you do?"

"I do."

I stretch my arms behind my head, trying to seem more confident than I am. Like I know what's going on here, like I'm totally sure it's going to be fine. My top inches up just a little. He reaches out and pulls down the hem, but leaves his fingers there, brushing just above my hipbones, running them back and forth.

"Enlighten me."

"A part of you wants me."

I roll my eyes. "I'm serious, Drew."

"So am I. A part of you, a small part, or maybe a huge one, wants to be with me. But your Daddy issues are making it impossible, so you stay away and then don't understand when you can't handle a girl spending the night with me."

"That is so not true, you narcissist."

His fingers stop moving and rest there on my hip, and he just stares down at me. My heart is pounding faster and harder than it's ever pounded. With his other hand, he brushes a stray hair from my face behind my ear. I've always wanted a guy to do that. Wherever his fingers touch, my skin buzzes.

He lowers his face several inches, until I can feel the warmth of his face, see the moisture on his lips. I should want to leave. I don't like him, I don't. Not like that. But in this moment, the last thing I want to do is move away.

Then he looks me in the eye and whispers, his mouth so close I can feel the words on mine, "You're dying for me to kiss you."

I swallow hard and look away. Because if I keep staring at him and he doesn't kiss me, I think I *will* die.

"Don't worry," he says, still playing with my hair. "You don't need to worry around me. I won't kiss you. I'll never kiss you. Not until you ask me to."

The fact that he chose the word *until* rather than *unless* is glaring. And I can't say anything to combat it. I can barely breathe with him so close. He rolls off me and back onto the hood. After a few minutes with my vital signs, forcing them to calm down, I look over at him.

"I'm sorry. About being jealous. And about . . . everything else."

"It's okay." He slips an arm under my shoulders. "It's just complicated with you now."

"It never used to be complicated."

"Yeah, well, you never used to have boobs."

"Drew," I yell, and I hit him in the chest. He laughs hard and clutches the spot where I hit him.

"You gonna blog about that tomorrow? How to throw a mean right hook?"

I shake my head and lie there with him, as confused as I ever was, staring up at the stars. And he stares with me until we're ready to go home. I sleep over again. Because why not?

11. How to Bake Stuffed Mushrooms

I wake up the next morning, tiptoe out of Drew's room over to my house, and climb in my own window. Dad knows where I've been, but sometimes I still feel weird being brazen about it. Like I'm actively trying to piss him off, which I'm not, not really. Not always, at least.

So sneak I do. Minutes after I jump into my own bed, I get a text. It's from Seth. Even in my groggy, half-conscious state, I know to be excited about that. Seth Levine has my number.

Before opening the message, I fantasize that he's asking me out for a romantic evening, moonlit walk on the beach or something. It's probably just about the math tutoring. Failed another exam, most likely.

You want to come over tonight?

I pause and stare at the screen. That could mean just about anything. Do you want to come over tonight and talk about triangles? Do you want to come over tonight and get it on? Do you want to come over tonight and bake homemade cookies and sing "Kumbaya" and braid each other's hair? The phone buzzes again.

For cooking lessons. I owe you one.

Okay, so it's an Option 1/Option 3 hybrid. I can live with that.

Sure. It's a date.

Oh, eff. Why did I just send that? Is there such a thing as a Freudian text slip?

Cool. Pick you up around 6?

I feel the hypertension drain from my shoulders when he doesn't acknowledge my idiocy, and I breathe a huge sigh of relief.

See you then ☺

I can't stop smiling as I sit down at my computer to check my blog. I can barely even remember the password, I'm so flustered (in the best of ways).

On the third attempt, I finally enter the correct log-in and head straight to questions, sorting a few into the MAYBE folder and some straight into the trash. I don't care how much money it makes me, I have zero interest in learning how to make homemade baby food or how to stash a body. (Though I consider, momentarily, trying to find the IP address of whoever posted that . . .)

Tonight, I'll tackle a cooking question or two, probably. Most of my fans, it seems, are looking for cooking advice, style tips, or various sexual tactics, ranging from the best way to give a memorable hug to, well, things that go in the trash. On that subject, I have to admit, I haven't written much. I haven't done much to write about. I'm hoping that will change sometime in the (near) future. Someone has *got* to want to kiss me eventually.

It doesn't take a giant leap from there for me to start daydreaming about Seth. Hands in my hair, lips on my neck or lips or anywhere. I bet he uses the perfect amount of tongue.

I fall back on my bed like a girl from one of those cheesy old movies Mom used to force me to watch, because sometimes you just have to be that girl. And right now, I am. My blog is going crazy. I've gotten hundreds of dollars already (which is insane), people—the right people—are finally starting to realize I exist at school, and I'm going over to cook at Seth's house. Seth, who I've had a distant celebrity-type crush on since I met him. Yeah, when you get to be that girl, even for a minute, you have to savor it.

So I do. Pretty much all day, I'm Tra La La Renley. Doing dishes without complaint, making sandwiches for everyone for lunch, chattering at Mach-10 about New York and the planetarium, smiling. My dad is thrilled with that, and so is Stacey. She probably takes it as a sign that I'm finally starting to accept her as my replacement mom. Any change of mood, Stacey believes, must have to do with her. Because teenagers live and die based solely on their relationships with their stepmothers. That annoys me enough that I almost want to start scowling again. But I don't. I'm too busy being *that girl*, and it's just too much fun.

By the time evening rolls around, I've changed my outfit six times and redone my makeup twice that. The doorbell rings at 5:59, which is the only thing that keeps me from changing again and redoing my makeup for the thirteenth time.

I thunder down the stairs before my dad can answer and stop at the door, panting, embarrassingly, from running for ten seconds. I'm a runner, dammit. This is ridiculous. I stand there for several seconds so I can calm down to a reasonable level, then open the door.

"Ready to go?" he asks.

"Sure."

I follow him across the yard and climb into his car for the second time in a week, and we drive off. He flips the radio on, and something cool and old school purrs through the speakers. He looks at me from the corner of his eye and grins. "You cool with this? Or do I need to change it to pop rap dance-house?"

I give him a look and turn up the volume.

"Oh good," he says. "I thought you were cool. That was the test."

"Well, I never fail. Otherwise, you wouldn't be paying for my tutoring in tasty treats."

"Never fail, huh? You and Mr. Cole getting along all of a sudden?"

"Besides cooking. Cooking is the exception to all things with me."

He laughs and turns as we near his subdivision. "Well, try not to burn my house down, if you would."

"I'll do what I can. But no promises."

"I'll try not to get us into any math-related emergencies in return."

We pull into his driveway and head to the front door. The lights are all off when we go inside.

"Are we here alone?" I ask.

"Yeah. Parents are dropping off my little brother at a friend's. They'll be back in a few. I wouldn't want your parents to think I was trying to corrupt their daughter or anything." He winks at me and heads over to the kitchen.

"Ha. Trust me when I tell you they wouldn't care."

I follow Seth to the sink and mimic him, dousing my hands with warm water and soap.

"So," I say, "what are we making?"

"I have everything for stuffed mushrooms here."

"Fancy." The thought of making stuffed anything is intimidating, since I have a difficult time reheating chicken nuggets. But I will power through.

Seth opens his refrigerator and pulls out myriad ingredients: mushrooms, bread crumbs, garlic, several kinds of cheese I can't really identify from here, and a few other things that get lost in the pile he sets on the granite island.

"That's like a hundred ingredients."

"Eh, more like fifteen." He shrugs and smiles.

"This is lesson one. You couldn't have started with pasta or something?"

"Oh come on," he says. "You're not the kind of girl to shy away from a challenge, are you?"

He raises his eyebrows and stares straight into my eyes, his glinting with mischief, which makes me go hot all over. An errant black curl falls over his eyebrow and he brushes it back.

"You're right," I tell him. "I *love* a challenge."

"Good." He starts to arrange everything in a more reasonable, less intimidating order, and I just lean on the island, propping my chin up with my hands. "Besides, if I'm teaching you, this is the way it's gonna be. No pasta or casserole or instant pudding mix. I don't do anything halfway." He steals another glance at me and grins, then pushes the pile of mushrooms at me.

"I can handle that," I say. I look down at the mushrooms. "So where do we start?"

"First thing you're gonna do is pop the caps off those mushrooms."

"It's like you're speaking a foreign language."

He laughs and crosses over to my side of the counter. "This," he says, pointing to the fat end, "is the cap." He flips it over. "This is the stalk. Just separate the two and hand the caps to me so I can clean them."

I grab one of the mushrooms and snap, and to my shock, it comes clean off. Something I can't screw up.

That was merciful of him. I separate the mushrooms quickly and toss them to him to wash, which he does lightning fast. Then he brings the bowl of caps back to me.

"Okay, so we're going to leave these alone for a while. Now comes the fun part." He hands me a knife—a giant, extremely sharp-looking knife. My eyes widen and I look frantically between Seth and the blade of death in my hand.

"I'm not going to stab you with it. Calm."

"No, no. I'm afraid *I'm* going to stab me with it."

He rolls his eyes. "You'll be fine." Then he steps around me and sweeps his arm across the mushroom stalks, pushing them all onto a cutting board. "Breathe. You will survive this," he teases, and I narrow my eyes. "Just chop these up and slide them into that skillet."

I eye the stalks like they're going to jump up and bite me. None of them do. Then I bring the knife down upon them, and one piece flies.

"Whoa, okay. Not like that. You're not trying to murder them. You already chopped their heads off."

I flush and bring the knife down again a little more gently. Once again, flying mushroom body parts.

"Yeah, you're starting to get a little stabby. Let me show you." He takes the knife from me and braces the cutting board with one hand and grips the knife firmly in the other. Then he sets the tip of the blade on the bamboo and chops from the handle, the tip never leaving the board. Frick, something about that is unreasonably hot.

And, of course, now a pile of perfectly chopped mushroom stalks is sitting there, taunting me.

He hands me the knife, and I make an attempt, but the stupid knife won't stay rooted to the board, and all I end up doing is moving mushroom pieces around.

"Close," he says. "Like this."

He puts his right hand over mine and his left on my shoulder, then lifts the handle of the knife, bringing it slowly down again, and then speeding until it's rocking and the mushrooms he's—*we're*—cutting are coming out perfectly.

His hand is warm and still damp from washing the mushrooms earlier, and I wish I didn't notice the gentle pressure of his left hand on my shoulder, the slight heat from his breaths beside my ear. He gently lets up on my knife hand and backs away, letting me take over. And I've totally got it now.

I pretend the pulse pounding all the way up in my throat is from the thrill of getting this right, not from him touching me. He has a girlfriend. He has a girlfriend.

"Beautiful," he says.

"What?" I drop the knife beside the cutting board and spin around.

"The stalks. They're beautiful."

"Oh. Yeah. Thanks."

He comes around me and takes the cutting board, brushing the chopped stalks into a skillet. "And now the really fun part," he says. He gestures for me to join him by the cooktop. Visions of third-degree burns and house fires rush through my head when he turns it on. He puts a little butter in the bottom and as it melts, he says, "Bring, well, everything else."

I transfer all the spices and random ingredients to the counter beside the cooktop and he steps back. "Okay, you're on."

I can feel the color drain from my face. "What do I do?"

"Toss in some of this. A little more. Good."

And the process goes like that for a while. I'm stirring and adding ingredients like I'm Gordon Ramsay. A little cheese, a little garlic, some bread crumbs.

"And the coup de gras." He hands me a bottle and I raise an eyebrow.

"Beer? So you're a rebel then?"

He smirks. "Maybe. Don't tell." I pour a little into the pan and he takes the bottle from me and drinks.

"Let's just implicate me too. That will guarantee my silence." I take the bottle back from him and put my lips around the rim, where his just were. Questions of what it would feel like to kiss him whirl around in my head and I take a swallow, and smile with my eyes. I take a swallow, thinking only about my mouth and his mouth and not at all about how much I hate beer, and when it touches my tongue, I cough. I have to physically force myself to swallow.

He raises an eyebrow when I give him a thumbs-up, then takes back the bottle. He leans up against the counter as I stir, taking another swig. I wonder if he can taste my cherry lip gloss, and how it combines with the flavor of the beer.

The pan is sizzling and popping and emitting the most amazing smell. Butter and garlic and mushroom and Heaven, basically. I inhale deeply and close my eyes, lost in the smell and the warmth in the kitchen.

Seth walks quietly to my side and takes the pan from the burner, then shuts it off. He sets it on a hot pad on the island, and hands me a spoon, taking one himself.

"So, you're just gonna spoon this stuff into the mushroom caps."

I sit across from him, still overwhelmed by the smells swirling around the room, filling every available crevice. Stacey, while apparently my father's dream girl, can't cook more than a box of cereal, so this is awesome.

I take a spoon and let it do lazy circles in the Heaven-mix, then start spooning it in. He does the same. We sit in silence, filling the mushrooms, then setting them on a baking pan and sprinkling them with cheese. Seth, wisely, takes the pan from me and puts it in the hot oven, undoubtedly saving my wrists from severe scarring.

"And now we just wait for about fifteen minutes."

"I can't get over how amazing this smells."

"Right? It's like, my anti-drug." He laughs. When he does, he leans over and shifts, and his chain falls from his shirt.

"What's that?" I ask, reaching over to grab the charm.

"Star of David. Mom got it for me when I turned seventeen last month. And the chain I got from . . . uh . . . Taylor." He looks away and I cough, dropping the star like it's on fire.

Neither of us says anything for an awkward minute, and I think we're both extremely grateful when his parents come bustling in the door.

"Seth, it smells *marvelous* in here!" his mom shouts. Her voice is round and lovely, and I can hear her smiling.

Both of them come around the corner into the kitchen and shrug off their jackets. His dad smiles a broad smile at me, holding out his massive hand for me to shake. I take it. They are both super beautiful. His dad is tall and giant with smiling eyes, and his mom is short and curvy, and her lips are perfectly bowed and pink. Both of them have the same amazing, tanned complexion as Seth.

"This is Renley," Seth says.

"Oh, the math friend you have. Great to meet you, Renley," says the dad.

Ugh. The math friend. Could I *be* any deeper in the friend zone?

I sit there for a while, forgetting the slight, and enjoy the cacophony I can't believe these two people can create themselves. The timer goes off on the oven but I can barely hear it over the sheer power of his parents' voices.

Seth goes to the oven and takes the mushrooms out, and waits about five loud minutes to hand a semi-cooled one to me.

"The moment of truth," he says.

I eye it and take a hesitant bite. But I immediately just stick the entire thing in my mouth because I have very little sense of decorum. It pops when I bite into it, cheese and mushroom and spices melting everywhere. I actually moan a little when I taste it. That would be embarrassing except that I'm sure no one can hear me.

"This is amazing," I sigh.

Seth pops a whole mushroom in his mouth and nods, eyes lighting up.

"Not bad for your first lesson."

"Not bad?" I scoff.

"Not bad. I say, you pass." He winks at me again and I go for another mushroom, hoping he fails at trig forever and I never get any better at cooking.

12. How to Make Out

I sit at my computer desk, shaking my leg so hard things are rattling and falling off it to the floor. The nail on my index finger is chewed down to the quick. I've been thinking about Seth for the last few days, sure. I mean, how could I not? A hot cooking night has been everyone's fantasy since all those movies in the eighties decided that food was sexy. But that's not what's got me going crazy.

There's a question lighting up on my blog, a question that's been there for ages. I wanted to delete it the second I saw it, but I couldn't. Probably because it's one of the top searches on Google, and an answer from a "certified expert" on this subject would rake in enough money to get me halfway to New York. I might even be able to charge two bucks to access the answer to this one, instead of the usual.

It would be worth it. I wake up my phone and start typing, and then, like I've done over and over for the past several hours, I shut it down again. This is ridiculous. I'm not twelve. I just need to put on my big-girl panties and text him.

After several more failed text attempts, I finally work up the nerve.

How to Make Out

Can I come over?

I click SEND before I can force myself to think about it. Seconds later, Drew texts back.

Duh.

I stand up so fast I knock over all the remaining small items on my desk, then I run my fingers through my hair to give it an ounce of body. Before I leave, I toss a piece of gum in my mouth for good measure. Fine, two pieces of gum.

I power-walk over to Drew's place and knock on the door, refusing to let myself consider what I'm about to ask him to do, or what it could change or, well, anything related to the situation.

He answers the door looking totally normal, which is absurd to me.

"Whoa. You okay?" he asks, a smile in his voice.

"Yes, Drew. I'm fine," I snap. I don't even know why I'm pissed. I'm probably not, not really.

I push past him into the foyer and he keeps his distance.

"Let's go downstairs. My room is trashed." That's code for *I've got another girl's underwear on my floor and I'd rather avoid that whole situation.*

I take a couple steps in front of him and lead the way downstairs. Every time we're down here, I wonder why we don't always hang out here. His basement is finished and carpeted and huge and totally spotless. Better than a dirty, cramped room that smells like boy. Anyway, who cares about that right now?

I go straight to the corner and sit, picking at my nails and chewing my gum furiously, refusing to look at Drew.

"Seriously, R," he says when he sits in front of me, cross-legged, "you're acting really weird."

"I need a favor from you."

"Okaaaay . . ."

I take the gum out of my mouth and toss it in the trash nearest to me. Then I take a deep breath. "I need you to teach me to do something."

"Is this for your blog? I have a plethora of ties stashed in my room."

"No, it's not that."

He looks at me quizzically, and I don't elaborate. Then he says, "Spit it out, girl. What do you need? I'm yours."

I finally look up at him. "I need you, um . . . this is so stupid. I need you to teach me to make out."

His jaw drops. "Are you serious?"

I stand. This was a ridiculous idea. "Never mind. This is stupid. I need to go home."

He catches my wrist and looks up at me, tugging gently. "No, stay."

I slowly sit and look at him, though I'd like to be looking *anywhere* else.

"So you need to teach your loyal readers how to suck face, and you're asking my expertise?" He wiggles his eyebrows, teasing me like this isn't totally embarrassing.

"That's disgusting. And yes. I am. I don't have anyone else to ask."

"Not even April? I bet she'd help you out. Invite me over."

I hit him in the chest and he falls back, laughing. "Seriously though, you have to become a 'certified expert' on this topic? Have you ever even kissed a guy?"

I scoff. "I'm sixteen. Of course I have."

He scoots a little closer. "With tongue?"

I purse my lips and look away.

"That's what I thought. Maybe you should just let me ghostwrite this one for you."

I pause for a second, considering that. He's kissed the equivalent of like the entire population of a small country by now, so maybe . . . No. I need to do this myself. I roll my eyes at him and say, "Okay, enough. Are you going to do it or not?"

The little smirk on his face reduces and he looks me in the eye. "So you're asking me then. To kiss you."

I draw in a shaky breath. "Yes."

He scoots closer to me and moves his face toward mine. I find myself inching backward. "What are you doing?" I blurt out.

"I'm gonna kiss you."

I move back closer to him and he leans forward, not touching me anywhere. And when he kisses me, it's like that scene from *Sixteen Candles*. Mom made me watch it a couple months before the blow-up and she was totally embarrassed when she remembered it had boobs and an f-bomb. Anyway. That doesn't matter. Drew is kissing me. *Sixteen Candles*. It's like that scene where Molly Ringwald and Jake Ryan lean over the birthday cake. It's a small kiss, almost innocent, and it doesn't send shivers down my spine or anything.

He pulls back and grins, licks his lips a little. "Green apple gum. Interesting choice."

"Shut up."

"I just need to say one thing before I kiss you again."

"Shoot," I say.

"I'm . . . you know I'm in love with you. That's not a state secret. So if I get caught up in this, if I go too far, anything, I need you to tell me. Because I'm being honest with you here. I might, if I'm kissing you, I might start thinking with my dick, and it does not know I'm doing this for a blog."

"Eloquent."

"I'm serious."

"I know," I say. "And I trust you. You go too far, I'll tell you."

"Okay."

We both sit there in silence for a minute, then he inches even closer than he was before.

"I'm gonna kiss you again. And I'm gonna use tongue."

I steady myself; my heartbeat is wildly out of rhythm. "Okay."

He leans forward, slowly this time, and I can see that he's shaking. And then he kisses me, soft at first, just his lips on mine. This time—maybe because it's real, maybe because I know what's coming—I get tingles everywhere. Then he nudges my mouth open with his and there's a tongue. There's a guy's tongue in my mouth. What am I supposed to do with this? Oh no. Do I lick it or something? I don't even think there's room for me to move mine. I think maybe I'm biting it a little. This is not good. Mayday. Mayday. And then he slides his hand up my leg and I jump so far back, I hit my head on the wall.

He jumps back, too, like I've stuck him with a cattle prod.

"You touched my leg. Your tongue was in my mouth. Drew, you freaking, you licked my mouth."

"I did *not* lick your mouth."

"Well, I don't know what else you'd call it. And what was that? With your hand?"

"Excuse me," he says, clearly annoyed. "Sorry for touching you while we made out. I apologize; I usually touch a girl with something other than my lips when I kiss her. It's not like I was fondling you."

I shake my head. "This was such a bad idea."

"No it wasn't. You just need to chill out."

"I need to chill out? Okay Shaky McGee, master of tongue. You're the one giving me semi-rapey pre-kiss warnings and *I'm* the one who needs to chill out."

He narrows his eyes. "I'm going to ignore that for now, and teach you how to kiss a guy, okay? You're overthinking it. When I kiss you, you're thinking about where your tongue should go and if this is exactly how it's supposed to feel, and *Oh no, his fingers are touching me in completely appropriate places.* Just stop. Stop thinking about it and let me kiss you."

The crazy pulse again. Now I'm shaking. He brushes a lock of hair behind my ear and runs his fingers through it with one hand, while he slips the other just under the hem of my shirt, to my bare waist. Then he inches closer to me, so close that I can't believe we're not kissing yet. He just lingers there for a minute until I can feel myself moving toward him, wanting to kiss him.

When our lips touch, it's me who brought them together. But Drew takes control fast, pulling my head toward his, fingers tangled in my hair. This time, when he slides his tongue between my lips, I just let it happen. I try not to think, try not to analyze everything, just let myself feel the rush of it, the intoxicating touch of his fingers in my hair, him gripping my lower back, his mouth moving against mine.

He pushes me back against the wall lightly, and when I reach out and let my fingers play at the base of his scalp, he breathes out a low sound and pulls me closer. And that's when I know I have to stop. I don't want to. But I do, pushing gently at his chest.

He sits back, and I swallow hard, just staring at him.

"Not bad for your first time," he finally says, his mouth smirking, but his eyes looking almost pained.

"Oh thanks. You sure know how to compliment a girl."

"Maybe not, but I know how to kiss one."

I laugh, mostly because I have to find some way to release the tension pent up in me, like a spring dying to uncoil.

"I think we're done for today," he says, and he stands up, turning his back to me.

"Where are you going?"

"Cold shower."

He walks up the stairs without another word, but I just sit there for a while, analyzing it all, feeling it all again. I won't post on it for a while. I'm not there, not after one make out session. But I'll be back, asking for another lesson. That's stupid, I know. But I will, because sometimes, I'm stupid.

13. How to Get Invited to the Biggest Party of the Semester

I wake up with the feel of Drew on my lips. Ever since yesterday, I haven't been able to stop thinking about it. It's not that I have real feelings for Drew—it can't be. Or at least it shouldn't be. I am seriously stupid. I cannot be feeling anything for Drew, considering he's probably waking up next to a new half-naked coed again this morning. It's just probably because he was my first actual kiss. Any girl would be feeling the same way (and with him, probably a hundred girls have).

Still, I lie in my bed, running my fingers over my lips, rehashing the whole thing over and over, wondering if I should have done things differently, if he thought it sucked, if he liked it. I lie there forever, refusing to drag myself out of bed, till my phone vibrates.

It's probably Drew. Maybe April, confirming our plans for tonight. I roll over slowly and grab it off my nightstand, and when the screen lights up, I see it's Seth. For the second time in just a few days, he's woken me up with a text. I pinch myself, just to be totally sure I'm not

112

still asleep. I'm not sure what that's supposed to do; I heard once it's because you don't feel pain in dreams, but that's a load of bullcrap if I ever heard one. Either way, I pinch myself, and come to the conclusion that I'm not dreaming.

Hey Renley—you free tonight?

Yeah. Why?

One of Taylor's friends is having this huge bonfire. Thought you might want to come.

I blink dumbly. Since when do I get invited to bonfires not held by the math club?

What time? I send back, trying to be cool.

After dark. Down by the lake. You interested?

I'm in. I don't have a ride though. :-/

That's fine. I'll come by.

Sweet. See you then.

I sit up in bed, totally awake now. I'm going to a bonfire tonight. By the lake. With a bunch of kids everyone knows, but nobody *knows*. After tonight, though, I will. And that feels kind of awesome.

I jump out of bed and throw my hair in a messy pony-tail, then bound down the stairs to the breakfast table.

"Oh hey there, Leelee!" Stacey says, giant smile painted on her face. How she's managed to keep that thing on perpetually for the last five years is beyond me. I'm almost impressed, to tell the truth. "You're up super early this morning."

"Yeah." It's not that early; it's after ten. She's just not used to actually seeing me before noon, when I'm forced to come out of hiding and socialize.

"Want me to make you breakfast?"

What's she gonna make me? A pop-tart? "Uh, sure. What do we have?"

She walks over to the pantry, miniscule hips swaying back and forth like a Real Housewife. "Cap'n Crunch, Mini Wheats, and Kix."

"Kix," I say, leaning back in my chair. I'm usually a do-it-yourself kind of person, but when it comes to Stacey, I'll take pretty much whatever she offers, which is a lot. Other Woman, Sorry I Wrecked Your Family and Forced Your Mom to Abandon You guilt. Fine by me.

I clasp my hands behind my head and stare off into the distance, bonfire-related dreams filling my mind. Stacey comes over and sets a bowl and spoon in front of me, then grins knowingly (like she's really old enough to have garnered a wealth of parental wisdom).

"I know that look," she says, voice rising and falling like a song.

"What look?" I coat my Kix with milk and take a bite, crunching obscuring what she says, just slightly. I crunch a little louder.

"You have a boy."

I groan.

"It's fine! I mean, it's great!" she says. "I remember my first real crush. I was in the ninth grade—"

"Which was, what? Two or three years ago?" I mumble under my breath.

She freezes and swallows, then carries on like she hasn't heard what I said. "I was in the ninth grade, and he played on the baseball team. So cute. He kissed me once."

She leans on the table, chin resting on her palms, and smiles.

"That's awesome," I say drily, and I shovel the rest of my cereal in my mouth.

"Anyway, I'm just saying it's nice."

I don't say another word to her. Sometimes I forget that she's a morning person and make the mistake of emerging from my room too early. Then there's not even Dad to act as a buffer between us. It's torture. I head back upstairs the second my bowl is empty and leave her alone in the kitchen, standing there awkwardly, an empty cereal bowl in her hands.

When I get to my room, I see a couple missed calls on my phone, both from April.

I dial her number quickly, and she picks up on the first ring.

"Hey, love!" she says, too chipper for any hour designated "a.m."

"Hey, lady."

"So, we on for tonight?"

"Oh man. We were hanging out tonight? I totally thought it was tomorrow," I lie.

There's a little pause on the other end. Then, "You did? Even though it's Sunday night and we have tomorrow off school for once? You thought I was spending the night on Monday? Before school the next morning."

The sarcasm in her tone makes it exceedingly clear she does not believe me.

"I seriously did. It's just . . . I have this thing tonight."

"What kind of thing?"

"With Seth."

She puts this fake excited voice on and says, "Ooooh, Seth again? I don't blame you. He's probably a lot more fun to make out with than me."

"I'm not making out with him."

"Still a mouth virgin?" she says, clicking her tongue at me. I don't feel like correcting her, for some reason. "You know, if you don't fix that problem soon, your tongue is gonna shrivel up."

"I'll bet."

"I'm just telling you what I read."

There's an awkward silence before she asks, "So, maybe I could just come over after?"

"The thing is, I don't know how long I'm going to be out."

"Oh," she says. "Okay. Fine. I'll see you lat—"

She hangs up before I can hear the end of the last word, and a trickle of guilt makes its way into my stomach. I shouldn't blow off plans with April to go flirt with some guy who has a girlfriend. But she would totally do the same in my shoes.

No, she wouldn't.

But I can't think about her all day; it'll kill the amazing night that's coming. So I stop and distract myself with the computer and homework and weird hair and makeup until darkness falls.

♂

Stacey gets to the door before I do, and she opens it for Seth. I hear him introduce himself, his voice muffled through the door as I walk down the stairs.

"I'm Renley's mom," she says, and the hair on my arms stands up. She thinks I didn't hear her? I stare darkly at the side of her face until she glances over and sees me, then shoots me a bright, approving look. Clearly, Seth is her type. I continue glaring silently until her face falls and she corrects herself. "Stepmom. Renley's stepmom."

She shakes his hand and I step around the open door and into Seth's view. He smiles.

"You ready to go?"

"Born ready."

I grab a light coat from the coat closet and breeze out the door, Seth on my arm.

"You'll have to sit in the back, if that's okay."

I nod and glance at his car. His passenger's seat is very occupied by Taylor, a fact that makes my insides wilt. But I get inside the car anyway and fake a smile.

"Hey, Renley, you made it!"

"Hi, Taylor." Despite desperately wanting to hate her automatically, it gives me a thrill to hear her use my name. It doesn't really make sense, but the celebrity of it all, it's cool to know that someone *everyone* knows knows you. A hint of genuineness enters my smile and I lean back in the seat.

Seth gets in the driver's seat and the car glides away toward the lake. He turns up the music the second he gets in, making the silence less uncomfortable. I wonder if that was for my benefit, or for his and Taylor's. I notice fleetingly that their elbows don't even touch, though they're both resting them on the middle console.

Then I look out the window to distract myself from dumb speculations that'll lead to nothing but me getting disappointed.

I don't live far from the lake, so the drive goes by pretty quickly. I can see the bonfire when we're still a minute away, and when we get closer, I can hear the bass thrumming through the walls of the car. It clashes heavily with the music Seth's radio is blasting, which is kind of disorienting.

I jump out of the car when we get there and find myself surrounded by a throng of people I definitely recognize. Taylor skips off, presumably to find a gaggle of her friends, and Seth watches her leave, then turns to me.

"Can I get you a beer or something?"

I look around and see that most of the kids have red plastic cups in their hands. "Thanks, but I'm good. This feels more illegal than sipping a beer in your kitchen."

He laughs. "Yeah. I'm DD, so we can be sober together."

He takes a couple steps over to the cooler and digs through the ice, pulling out two cans of Dr Pepper. He hands one to me and I smile to myself. He remembered.

"Come on," he says. "I'll introduce you to a couple of my friends."

I follow him to a spot close to the fire, where a group of extremely attractive kids is sitting. Seth takes a place on a half-crowded log and I sit next to him, trying to ignore the smoke burning my eyes.

He leans over and shoulder bumps a girl next to him.

"What are you guys looking at?"

"*Sweet Life*. It's a blog."

"Oh yeah, I've heard of that. Taylor's addicted to it."

My eyes widen so hard, I think they might pop out of my head. Taylor Krissick reads my blog. And so does everyone else who matters around here, apparently. This is insane.

The girl looks up from her smartphone and smiles at me. She's pretty, like everyone else on the log, with dark hair, dark skin, huge eyes.

"Who's your friend?" she asks Seth.

"This is Renley. She's basically saving my life in trig."

"Hey, I'm Sam," she says.

They go down the line, a blonde called Emily, a curvy girl named Sophie, and one who's super tall named

Ash. No one seems to notice that I don't belong here. I stare around the circle and think about it and maybe it's because I *do* belong here for once.

Lots of girls in waterfall braids and coats, sipping soda from a can. I do fit in. I relax on the log and Seth flips around to talk to a couple guys and I fiddle with the tab on the Dr Pepper can.

"Do I know you?" someone with a deep voice asks beside me.

I turn to see who. No, we don't know each other, but I definitely recognize him. He's on the football team. "Gary Harding?"

"Yeah, and you're . . ."

"Renley."

"Oh yeah, I've seen you around. Enjoying the party?"

I shrug. "Sure."

"It's kinda lame. But the beer's good."

I take a drink of Dr Pepper and he frowns and takes it from me. That ticks me off right away.

"What are you doing drinking this? Let me get you a beer."

Yeah. I might be learning how to do a lot of things, but this is one thing I already know: taking an open drink from some douchebag at a party is an absolute no. No thank you.

I make a move to snatch the soda back and he holds it just out of my reach.

"I'm not a big drinker."

"Oh come on. It's a party."

"Seriously, give me back my drink."

"Are you for real—"

Just like that, a hand grabs Gary's wrist, and Seth has stood up. He's way skinnier than Gary, but he's got a good couple inches on him, height-wise.

"Hey. Dick weed. Hands off."

Gary furrows his brow at Seth and, without looking at me, hands me back my drink.

"This is none of your business, Seth."

"Yeah. Yeah it is. I brought her here. She's my business. *Hands. Off.*"

Gary mutters something vulgar under his breath and stalks off, and Seth relaxes.

"You okay?"

"Yeah," I say. "The thing most in danger there was my Dr Pepper."

"Still though."

I sit back on the log and sip my roofie-free beverage, staring at the fire while the girls beside me scroll through my blog on their cells. And Seth hangs pretty close to me for the rest of the night.

14. How to Really Piss Off Your Best Friend

I get home after 1 a.m. and, when Seth drops me off, I look over and see Drew sitting on his front porch. He looks up when we pull in, and in the vague light from his stoop, I can see him furrow his brow. He waves, and when Seth and Taylor drive away, I decide to join him on his porch instead of going inside.

"Hot date?" he asks, waggling his eyebrows.

"Not really."

I can tell that was not the answer he was expecting, not a firm enough denial.

"I was at a party," I explain.

"Ah. That on your list of things to blog about?"

"No. Seth just asked me to come, and I thought it would be fun."

His expression darkens a little. Not like he's mad, just . . . I don't know. "Seth Levine?"

"Yeah. I mean, it didn't mean anything. He's dating someone, so . . ."

He nods, but looks past me. "Yeah. That Taylor girl, right?"

He's not really listening when I confirm it.

"So, what are you doing out here at one o'clock in the morning?" I ask, hoping to change the subject.

He goes really quiet and points his thumb back toward his mom's room. When I go still, I can hear a high-pitched, rhythmic voice coming from that direction.

"Oh."

"Yeah. Super easy to sleep through."

I scoot closer to him. "You want to come over to my house?"

He chuckles and looks at me. "I think I'm pushing it with your dad enough by having nightly sleepovers with you at my own house."

"Oh come on. He's harmless."

"I don't know. It's the quiet, nice ones you have to watch out for."

I smile and bump his shoulder with mine.

"Well, you can come over if you want."

"No," he says. "It's cool. They'll be done in about twenty minutes anyway."

I nod. "Well, there's no sense in sitting in silence listening to it." I pull out my iPod, hand him an earbud, and turn on a track.

"Ugh, this is awful, R," he says, but he's grinning.

"You love it."

He cocks his head, listening, then says, fake-resigned, "I do."

We sit there for a little while like that, leaning against his door, listening to horrible, great music. Two songs in,

I feel his pinky twitch against my thumb. Then it slides over until they're overlapping. He steals a quick glance at me, but looks away when he sees me looking back.

Slowly, he glides the rest of his fingers over and presses them between mine, rubbing his thumb back and forth across my wrist. I don't stop him, though him holding my hand is almost more terrifying than when he kissed me.

We share the earbuds and hand-space for the next twenty minutes, until he pulls his fingers away and stares at me.

"Well, I'm, uh, gonna go inside. They're done now. So, yeah. Thanks for staying with me."

He's being weird. Because of Seth, maybe?

"Sure."

Drew goes in and shuts the door, and I go home, because he didn't invite me to stay.

I wake up to this: **Did you have fun last night?**

I stare at the message from April, my heart rate rising, and respond, fingers shaking.

Ya.

Good. Nice party?

I freeze, eyes fixed on the phone. It buzzes again.

I know you went to the bonfire. Thanks for inviting me.

I can actually hear my pulse going crazy in my ear.

I mean, Seth WAS there. So you didn't really lie. Thanks for that.

I'm sorry. I shouldn't have gone to a party with a guy over hanging out with you. I did have it planned already tho.

I feel a rush of guilt, lying to her again.

Sure you did

I'm starting to get mad. It might not be totally fair—I *am* lying to her—but it ticks me off that she would automatically *assume* I'm lying.

Fine don't believe me.

She doesn't respond for, like, five minutes, and I start to feel guilty.

I'm really sorry.

After another minute, she texts back:

Okay.

Do you want to come hang out tonight maybe?

Sure! she writes.

Seconds later, she texts again.

Oh no, wait. Cash and I are going to a random party. Sorry.

I slam the phone down on my bed and cross my arms, then fall into my computer chair, spinning around and around. How did she even find out? Stupid question. It was a huge party. There could've been a hundred people who would've told her.

This is ridiculous. I got a Dr Pepper, some huge meat-head trying to do who-knows-what to me, and some guy I have an obviously unrequited crush on who drove me around with his girlfriend. Exchanging that for a hugely pissed off April was, admittedly, a really sucky trade.

I get another text a few minutes later and almost don't answer it, but the thirty seconds I spend resisting just stress me out like crazy. So I pick it up. My pulse falls to a manageable rate when I realize it's Drew.

Busy today?

Nope. Wide open.

Let's go up to our spot. Work on your blog.

It sounds like a really good idea. Better than it should.

I'll be over in five minutes.

15. How to Make a Possibly Huge Mistake

I throw my hair up without even bothering to brush it and pull a bra and tank top over my head. Yoga pants and a light jacket, and that's about as fancy as I'm going to get today. Not like it's going to make a difference to Drew.

I walk out the door and over to Drew's window and rap lightly on it.

"You comin'?"

He opens the window and gives me a devilish smile. "Of course. Wouldn't want to let your readers down."

He climbs through his window and pushes it closed behind him (best way to get out of the house without having to deal with his mom) then pulls his keys out of his pocket. I hop in the car with him, surprised at how calm and collected I'm able to keep myself, all things considered. He starts the hunk of metal, and we sputter down the road.

He side-eyes me when we get close to the overlook. "Hey, you remembered your jacket this time."

"Well, yeah. You certainly weren't gonna give me yours."

"Nope. I am not a chivalrous man."

He shifts down and puts the car into park, and we get out. The breeze is crisp, and the air smells like fall. I'm suddenly glad he didn't ask me to come at night or sunset or anything otherwise considered make-outey. The sun is warm enough for just this hour that I barely need the jacket.

Drew crosses over to the backseat on my side of the car and pulls out the fuzzy blanket from forever ago.

"You and your blanket again. I feel scandalized," I say.

He rolls his eyes and folds the blanket under one arm, reaching out the other one and resting it on the small of my back. It's an intimate touch, almost possessive, but Drew and I have never been overly sensitive about where we're allowed to touch each other.

We walk together just a little ways away from the car, into the cover of the trees. There's this little place here, if you take the time to find it, that is perfect: flat, shady, covered with leaves that have been softened by the perpetual dew. Even in the fall, this one spot is humid, which takes some of the bite out of the cold. We've visited it many a time.

He hands the blanket to me when we get there. "One sec. I forgot something." And he runs off, leaves crunching beneath his feet. I spread out the blanket and sit, leaning up against the nearest aspen, not thinking much of anything. It's too peaceful here to allow the rest of the craziness in my life to seep in.

It doesn't take him long to get back; Drew's a fast runner. He comes back into the little grove with a couple thermoses in hand. I somehow missed them when they were in the car.

"Ooh, what's in these? Something meant to lower my inhibitions?" I tease him.

He sits down next to me and hands me one. "Maybe." His eyes are sparkling. "But I don't need trick substances to do that. You asked me to do this, flat-out, with none of that crap. I'm just irresistible."

I shake my head and bring the thermos to my lips. It warms my hands, and whatever is inside is still steaming. High-quality beverage container. When I taste it, I shouldn't be as excited as I am, but I'm totally thrilled.

"Cider. You brought me apple cider." I take another taste. He was telling the truth; it's not spiked.

"With a drizzle of caramel I melted in the microwave myself, I'd like to point out."

I laugh and drink again. Cider is like my crack. If he was planning on taking me out here to teach me to make out, this was an unwise choice. I don't know any guy who could get me to willingly pry my mouth away from it for any reasonable length of time.

We sit there for a while, drinking in silence, until he sets his down.

"So . . ."

"So . . ." I parrot back, only willing to remove the thermos long enough to speak a syllable.

"We gonna do this thing or what?"

I giggle. "You shouldn't have brought me this if you really wanted that to happen."

"See, I thought I was earning nice-guy points. I very rarely get those."

"Oh you've got them," I say between tiny drinks, "it's just there's no way you're getting this away from my lips anytime soon."

He narrows his eyes at me and sits cross-legged inches from me for a while, watching me drink, paying particular attention, I notice, to my mouth.

I lower the thermos a bit more than I generally do between sips, just once, and he moves faster than I've ever seen him move, snatching it away and tossing it to the ground in one fluid motion. Before I can react, he grabs the back of my head and pulls it toward him, meeting my mouth with his own.

Even if I wanted to overthink everything, I couldn't, not with everything his lips are doing to me. I make a high little sound of surprise and he pulls me closer to him, until my body is pressed against his. One hand is still knit in my hair, the other on the small of my back, and he doesn't have to hint to me to part my lips. They just do.

He explores every bit of my mouth, and this time it doesn't feel foreign. It feels—dizzying. And right. He tastes like cider—warm spice and apples and perfection. I move my lips, my tongue, with his, and I understand now why making out is such a big deal to everyone.

Before I'm ready, he pulls back and looks me in the eye, intense and focused and terrified. And I don't want to stop. I lean forward, totally high off of all the sensations rushing through my body, and kiss him. I'm grabbing at his jacket and he shrugs out of it, leaving it abandoned on the blanket, but it's not enough.

My hands find their way beneath his shirt, and I run my fingers over his stomach, his chest. He pulls back for just an instant, breathing shakily. Everything on him is trembling hard. But he kisses me again, deeper, forceful, and it steals my breath. And I steal his shirt, peeling it off, wanting to feel his skin. I climb on top of him, not thinking. Not letting myself care that this is *Drew*. That I can't be with him. That he could hurt me worse than anyone could. All I can let myself feel is his heart pounding against my palm, the urgency when he kisses me, everything I can't believe I've never gotten to feel until this moment.

He sighs, low and gravelly, into me, and flips us over until he is on top of me, kissing me deeply, greedily, like he'll never kiss anyone again. When I feel his fingers trailing up my bare stomach, I don't pull away. I don't want to. I want to let him.

I raise up just a little, to shrug out of my jacket, and he pulls back from my mouth. Slowly, questioning me with his eyes, he takes off my shirt. I could stop him at any time if I wanted to. But I don't. And when he reaches around to unclasp my bra, I let that happen, too. If he didn't do it, I think I would have.

I lie back on the blanket, feeling every twig, every leaf underneath it, with goose bumps all over my skin, from Drew, and from the cold. But he doesn't care about the goose bumps. He just sits there, breathing hard and staring at me like I'm the most beautiful thing that has ever existed. Tender. And hungry. And he kisses me again, slowly. It feels so different this time that I almost don't notice one of his hands sliding up to a part of me that my shirt has always covered.

Almost. But when something hard brushes against my leg, and his other hand starts playing at the waist-band of my pants, I notice. And when he breathes my name and goes to kiss me again, I'm suddenly terrified. Because as much as everything in me wants it, I can't do this. I can't.

I say, "Drew," into his kiss, and he pulls back from me. "What?"

"I . . . I can't. We can't."

He draws in a breath and blinks hard, like he's trying to make the world focus. Then he looks at me, really looks at me, and that glazed look disappears.

"Renley. Oh man, R, I'm sorry." He scrambles back-ward, guilt all over everything. "I shouldn't have . . . I didn't mean to . . . Dammit. I'm sorry—"

"Drew," I say, sitting up. "Stop."

He shuts up and stares at me, wide-eyed.

"I took *your* shirt off, remember?" I say.

He starts to relax, but just barely.

"This was just as much me as it was you. I just can't do this."

"No, I don't want you to," Drew says.

I recoil like he's just slapped me and a panicked look comes over his face.

"No, that's not what I meant. Of course I want to. But you're not ready for this. I don't want to be someone you regret."

"And I . . . I don't want to be another notch in your bedpost."

A look I've never seen on anyone travels across his features. Confusion, anger, and extreme sadness, all tangled into one. I immediately want to take it back.

"You," he says huskily, bringing a hand to my face, "you could *never* be anything to me but the person I love most in the world. You are everything. A notch in my bedpost?" He sits back, running his fingers through his hair, hard.

"That's not what—"

"It's okay."

We sit there in tense silence for a few seconds, and Drew puts on his shirt and jacket.

"Yeah, we should go," I say.

"Yeah. I just . . ." He pauses awkwardly, then looks pointedly downward. "I, uh, need a second."

"Oh." I look away, bright red.

"It's gonna be a lot longer than a second if you don't put a shirt on."

I'm totally horrified. I forgot I was topless. I put on my shirt and bra in a semi-panic and reach for the cider that's dripping from the thermos. I drink it to occupy myself while we wait, and after what seems like forever, he stands.

"Let's go," he says, and we get silently into the car and roll away from our spot.

It's uncomfortable. He's seen me halfway naked, and touched me places no one ever has, and I don't know how to feel.

"Don't hate me," I say.

"I don't hate you," he says through gritted teeth. But then he breathes out, "A *notch* in my *bedpost.*"

I look away from him, and then back to his face. "I didn't mean that. I know you would never treat me that way."

He slams on the brakes and swerves off the dirt road, shutting off the car. "Treat you *what* way, Renley? What exactly do you think I do with those girls?"

"Um."

"I don't lie to them. They know exactly what they're getting with me. I don't promise I love them and then kick them out five minutes after we screw. And I've never cheated on a girl. Ever. I don't know why you think I'm this terrible guy—"

"I don't—"

"Or why you think I'm not *worthy* of a relationship. But I am not your dad. I'm not your crazy mom either. I would never do that to you. I promise all those other girls one night. And I give it to them. And I promise you that I will never stop loving you. And I won't. Because I don't break my promises, whatever they are."

I can't even look at him when I say, "I'm sorry."

He tries to start the engine, but it just rolls over. And again. And again. "Shit," he says, voice harsh and clipped. Then he leans back. "This happens sometimes. Just wait about half an hour and it'll start magically working again."

"I'm sorry, Drew."

He turns his head to look at me. "I don't want you to be sorry. I want you to know what you're worth."

I choke back a cry when he says that, and my eyes moisten. He slides his seat back until it's as far as it will go. And he lets me climb into his lap and throw my arms around his neck and cry.

16. How to Kick an Apple Cider Habit

When I click PUBLISH, I feel weird, like I'm revealing part of myself I don't want to reveal. Not to anyone, but especially not to all of cyberspace. But it needs to be done. This is going to make me the vast majority of what I need to get to New York. So I tell the world how to make out, and hide behind the identity of SweetLifeCoach.

I can't stop thinking about Drew, which is frustrating. It's been days. I don't want to think about him. And I don't want to get sucked into remembering what it felt like to kiss him, what his hands felt like on my body. Even just lying there in the quiet remembering everything is addictive. And I can't.

Every time I remember what it was like, it's interspersed with knowing that I can't hold on to that forever. Right now, the way he is, what we have, I can do this. But if I let myself fall in love with him, eventually he will get bored. And he will leave.

I can handle not kissing him again, I think. But I can't handle having no one to hold me while I cry like a wimp about my mom or dad or evil stepmother or whatever. I can't lose that. I won't. So I'm not going to text him. I'm texting someone else.

How goes the trigonometry?

Abysmal, Seth responds.

Apparently, he's good at English.

You free? I ask.

Yeah. I'll come over.

See you in 30?

Sounds good.

I take the next half hour to get ready, making sure everything is perfect, and notice that my roots are starting to show. I wonder if I can get April to redo them for me or if I'll have to fix them myself. I can't really go to a salon. I'm not an expert on everything I say I'm an expert on, but I have some principles.

I pick up the phone to text April, but stop short. What if she wants to come now and I have to say, "Can't! Hanging with Seth!" We've hardly talked since I blew her off and I don't want to risk making everything worse. So I purse my lips, set the phone down, and wait.

I hear the doorbell ring and my dad answers it. I stay in my room at my desk, finishing up my makeup before he sees me. Just as I finish my cat eyeliner (which I'm awesome at now, by the way), Seth knocks softly on my bedroom door.

"Come in," I say, and I spin around when he walks in, knowing full well how rockin' my legs look in this tiny skirt. From the way his gaze flicks down to my ankles and back up, I think he knows it too.

He swings his backpack around and sets it on the floor, then sits down with it.

"Do you want anything to drink?" I ask. "I've got . . ."

He pulls two cans of Dr Pepper out of his bag and I smile, then wonder if maybe he thinks I like the beverage more than I actually do. I conclude he doesn't, because I've brought a bottle to cooking nearly every day since the class started, so it's a fair assumption.

I sit in front of him (carefully, attempting to avoid a wardrobe malfunction) and pop open the can, then take a drink. *I wish this was apple cider*, I think. But that line of thinking is dangerous. I want it to be Dr Pepper. I had enough cider the other day to last me through the year. *Lie.*

"Thanks," I say, taking another drink, because no matter how much I'm craving apples and spice, this soda is good.

"No problem."

He unzips his backpack and pulls out his trig book and notebook, then lays them out on the floor.

"So, what are we going over today?" I ask him.

"This."

"Oh yeah. Trig terminology sucks. You kind of have them all screwed up everywhere."

He stares at the paper blankly, and I go into a lengthy, boring explanation of cosines, sines, and tangents.

He blinks at me.

"These are basically just formulas you have to memorize. Like, in cooking, you just know three teaspoons equals one tablespoon. You don't have to think about it. You don't have to understand it. Just memorize it."

"I can do that."

And we spend the next, like, fifteen minutes going over different sides of the triangle and where they are and which term they belong to. It's a triangle; there are only three. So how we spend that amount of time boggles my mind. He just really sucks at math.

Then again, these were probably the thoughts going through his head when I didn't know what a mushroom cap was. So.

After going around in circles (ironically) for fifteen minutes, Seth slams the notebook down and I jump. "My brain is dead," he says.

"I'm not going to argue with you."

He makes a face at me. "I didn't think tutors were allowed to belittle their students. Not good for their fragile self-esteems."

"I expect full vengeance next time we cook."

"Prepare yourself," he says, grinning. Then he stands. "You wanna get out of here?"

I stand with him, already heading toward the door, then hesitate. "I don't know."

He frowns.

"It's just—and this is gonna be a little awkward—you have a girlfriend."

The frown disappears from his face and he shakes his head. "Not exactly true."

And, cue heart in throat. "You don't?" I somehow croak, past the vital organ now blocking my trachea.

"No. We broke up a few nights ago. Actually, the night of the bonfire. After I dropped you off."

"Oh," I say.

"In all honesty, I wouldn't be over here right now if we hadn't called it quits."

I just stand there, frozen. There are very few reasons that could be true. "Why would that make a difference?"

"Come on," he says.

Nothing. My brain is giving me no material to work with, word-wise.

"You're gonna make me say it?"

Blank. It's like I've been lobotomized.

"I like you, Renley."

"You do?" I finally manage, because I had to say *something*.

"It's not why we broke up, though, I swear. Taylor and I have been over forever. So don't like, feel bad, or anything. And I don't want you to be under pressure, like you owe me a date or something. We would have broken up that night whether or not you and I had started hanging out."

My mind is a crazy place to be right now. Lots of information that I have no clue how to deal with. At all.

"I'm not asking you out right now, either. If that makes a difference. I'm just hungry, and I thought you might want to come with me."

Add slight embarrassment to the growing list of conflicting emotions.

"I, uh, sure. Let's eat something."

He leaves his stuff on my floor and we both head out. My dad catches my eye when we leave, and I see nothing but bright, shiny glee all over his face. He's thrilled, no doubt, that I've made an attractive male friend who is not Drew. This irritates me more than it should, but I brush it off and head across the lawn with Seth.

I climb into his car and notice right away that the candy smell is gone, replaced by something citrusy.

"I'm beginning to think you secretly do shop at Bath and Body Works," I say, inhaling the tropical scent.

He chuckles. "That's me. I have a secret stash of vanilla-scented body lotion hidden away in my room."

"Ew."

"Really though, I just didn't want the smell of Taylor all in my car. Gumdrop was too much." He looks over at me, then back to the road. "I did make a one-time trip to Bath and Body Works for it, though. I'm not gonna lie."

I shake my head. We pull in to one of those old-fashioned burger places, the ones where you pull up to a parking spot and people come out on roller skates to give you your food.

We sit there for a little bit, contemplating, and I eventually settle on a double cheeseburger, onion rings, and a chocolate malt. I'm too young to worry about calories and heart attacks.

It's not long till the food gets here; that's the nice thing about these in-between fast food/real food places. Moderately quick food restaurants. When the skater rolls up to Seth's window, he holds out enough cash for both of us, so I just sit there, a wad of cash in my hand, held out in front of his face.

"I got it. Don't worry about it."

The waiter takes it and hands him his change, then trades it for our food. After she leaves, but before I take a bite, I shove the cash into one of his palms.

"This is not a date. You don't need to pay."

He hands the money back. "Seriously, it's not a big thing."

I roll my eyes. "Seth. Take it. You ask me out on an actual date, I will happily let you pay. But not today."

He sighs and takes the money, but not before he encloses my fingers in his hand. He lets go quickly, so I don't even know if it was on purpose, but my fingers feel like it was.

"This car is kind of cramped," he says, opening the door. I follow his lead. He sits on the hood and holds out his hand, expecting me to join him. I take it, then stop. It just feels weird, the thought of sitting on the hood of his car, eating, talking about life or whatever. Like, this is Drew's and my thing. I don't know if sitting on a car can really be someone's thing, but it feels like it is.

"I think I'll just stay down here," I say, not sure why I feel guilty.

"Suit yourself." He takes a bite of his fries, and then says, "So. Hypothetically, if I did ask you out on an actual date, what would you say?"

I lean back against the car and take a sip from my malt, considering. But in that fatal drink, I get a piece of hardened malt, the kind that tastes awesome, but does not do good things if you suck it down your windpipe. I choke and my eyes water, coughing and sputtering and gagging.

"Whoa, never mind."

"No," I rasp. "Wrong . . . pipe . . ."

"Oh I hate that. You okay?"

I cough a couple more extremely attractive times and straighten again, setting the killer malt aside. "I'm fine."

I take a moment to catch my breath, then look over at him. "I'd say yes."

A smile spreads across his face. "You would?"

"I would. Hypothetically."

"Maybe I will then."

"Maybe you should."

My stomach flutters pleasantly when he stops for a minute, then says, "Hey, Renley, do you have plans on Saturday?"

"I don't. Why ever would you want to know?" I bat my eyelashes, teasing.

"I know this great little place I'd love to take you."

"It's a date."

17. HOW tO GEt a GUY tO GIVE YOU HIS PIN

Seth shows up at about seven, hair lightly gelled, hanging around his face in perfect ringlets it would take me five hours to achieve. Gelled hair, a henley tee, and a short-sleeve blue shirt over it. Letterman's jacket over that. He looks good. When does he not?

"You look nice," he says.

I blush. It took me forever to get looking this way, picking the perfect jeans, the shirt that makes me look the hottest. It's nice and really strange to have him compliment me.

I hear my dad walking up behind me. "Seth," he says.

"Mr. Eisler."

I can tell my dad is still completely in love with him from the way his eyes light up and his face is halfway covered by a giant smile. I don't blame him.

"Have her home before midnight."

I have a hard time not scoffing audibly. Dad wouldn't do a thing if I wasn't back until 5 a.m. But Seth doesn't know that. He just smiles and shakes my dad's hand.

"Of course," he says. "Ready to go?"

"Yup."

I go out the door with him, practically bouncing with every step.

"So, where are we going?"

He starts his car and we roll down the street. "I thought we could go to the Fall Fest downtown."

"Awesome."

We get closer and closer to downtown, and I'm so excited I can't believe it. Romantic date at the Fall Fest with Seth. This has the potential to be the best Saturday night I've had in maybe ever.

He parks in the first spot we see and opens my door for me, something Drew never thinks of doing, but that I find really attractive. Drew. Who cares if Drew would think of doing that? I'm here with Seth.

The sounds of polka music are drifting down Main Street, faint now, but I'm sure they'll get deafening when we get closer to them. Seth slips his hand around mine and a little thrill courses through my arm.

"Is this your kind of music?" I ask.

"What?"

"You obviously don't approve of my sugary pop rock, so I wonder if this is more your style."

He laughs loudly and starts toward one of the vendors. "Not exactly." He bumps me with his elbow. "And your sugary pop rock is fine."

I grin and we make our way to someone selling something that smells amazing.

"Ooh, glazed walnuts," Seth says, a look on his face that borders on lustful. "My favorite thing ever. Have you had them?"

"Nope," I say, but judging by the smell, I wish I had.

His eyebrows shoot up. "Seriously? Never? And here I thought we could be friends."

"Don't give up on me just yet. I'm willing to give them a shot."

He hands the vendor a couple bucks and pours some of the warm walnuts in my hands. I pop one in my mouth and *wow*. He was right. These and cider would be my most perfect meal. Screw the diabetes that would inevitably follow.

"Toss me one," he says, and we make our way to the middle of the street.

"Like, to your mouth?"

"Yeah." His eyes are twinkling and he takes a step or two back, still holding my hand.

I toss one in the air, and he stops with his mouth right where it's falling, then catches it on his tongue. I giggle, and throw another one, which he catches expertly.

"Impressive."

He smiles.

"Okay," I say, "you gotta go for three."

He drops my hand, and backs up, rubbing his hands together, expression extremely serious, like he's pumping himself up to pitch a no-hitter.

"Let's do this," I say. "The moment of truth."

I throw the nut and he opens his mouth, trying to get under it. But my trajectory was way off and it whacks him right in the eye. He jumps back and rubs his eye hard.

"Oh no!" I head over to him, stifling a laugh.

"That was on purpose. Any guy can catch food with his *mouth*. How many do you know who could catch it with their corneas?"

"Very remarkable."

"Thank you, thank you," he says, laughing, and mock bowing. There's still a trace of sugar around his eye and he keeps twitching it, which makes me feel kind of bad. But mostly it's funny.

He takes my hand again, warming my palm, and we walk down the street together, taking in the bad music and the smells of baking nuts and spices and funnel cakes and beer. He's running his thumb along my wrist, which is so hot.

"So, your dad seems nice," he says.

"Yeah. I'm pretty sure he's got a man-crush on you."

"Not quite sure how I feel about that."

"He's just glad I'm going out with a nice guy."

Seth raises an eyebrow. "Oh no, a nice guy. That's the kiss of death."

"No, no. It's good."

"And your dad's so thrilled because you usually go for the bad boy type? I can totally get a tattoo. Maybe even a piercing." He smirks.

I roll my eyes, trying not to think about the reason my dad thinks I'm into not-nice guys, which is not true at all. "Bad boys aren't my type. I'd rather hang out with guys who aren't gonna cut me open with a lip ring when they kiss me, or try to take my drink and spike it when I'm not looking."

He scowls. "So Gary Harding wouldn't be your type then."

"Ha. No."

"Sorry about that guy, by the way. I still feel kind of bad about that, since I invited you to the bonfire and all."

"It's fine. He's just a moron. Moron bad boys are *definitely* not my type. I like nice guys."

"And am I a nice guy?"

I smile and toss another walnut in my mouth, then walk ahead of him down the street. He laughs.

"Ooh!" I shout, pointing way ahead of us. "Ferris wheel. You want to ride?"

"Absolutely."

I walk more quickly, eager to make it to the ride, partially because I've always wanted to ride a Ferris wheel with a guy, and possibly just to get stuck for a while at the top.

When we get there, he hands the guy a couple dollars and we get in. The seats are open air, leaving us exposed, but it's worth it. It's dark outside and the lights of the city and the Fall Fest are twinkling everywhere. It would have been a crime to obscure that view.

After stopping a few times to let other people on, the ride slowly spins. We get higher and higher and everything looks more beautiful the longer the ride goes.

"It's amazing up here," I breathe, surveying the landscape below, the light glinting off the water nearby.

"Yeah. Some view."

I look at him when he says that and see that he's not looking at the city; he's looking at me.

"Shut up," I say, smiling, and hit him in the chest.

He turns up a corner of his mouth and looks out over the water. "I was talking about the lights."

"Mmhmm."

The wheel spins slowly and he inches closer to me, arm around my shoulders. It's pretty impressive; I don't even remember him putting it there.

And on the fourth go-round, it slows until it stops at the top, seat rocking gently back and forth. We are quiet for a second, and I can feel his gaze on the side of my face. I turn toward him, not realizing just how close together we were until now.

His fingers move gently on my shoulder, and my eyes are locked on his. Then he says quietly, "Can I kiss you?"

My palms instantly break into a sweat, and I'm glad he's not holding one. I nod, and he moves closer to me, eyes closing just before mine do. And then he kisses me, soft and sweet and slow, fingers still tracing circles on my arm. Chills spread from my lips to everywhere else, and he pulls back.

The ride is nearly over, and though the air is getting chilly, I'm completely warm.

We get off the Ferris wheel and he's holding my hand again, swinging it just slightly as we walk.

The night is getting darker, which is so romantic, but it brings with it a bite in the air. I shiver, the warmth of his kiss wearing off. I wish, like I always do, that I'd brought a heavier jacket. He looks over at me, noticing the shudder, and shrugs off his own coat, throwing it over my shoulders.

"Thanks," I whisper.

We spend the next couple hours just talking and eating and kissing occasionally, until he checks his phone and we notice the time.

"I've gotta get you home."

"Yeah. I mean, my dad's not going to care either way, but . . ."

"Still. I'd rather be on his good side."

I don't tell him that my dad's bad side is nothing to fear; I just go with him to his car. When he drops me off, it's 11:55, and I'm not ready to leave. He walks me to the front door, still holding my hand, and I break from it to take off his jacket.

"No, you keep it."

I turn it over, taking a real look at it. It's his letter jacket. I feel like I should be wearing a poodle skirt all of a sudden and laugh, donning a Southern Belle's accent. "Oh gracious. A boy givin' me his letter jacket. I wonder if he'll give me his pin."

He rubs the back of his head, flushing and smiling. "Only if you wanna go steady," he fires back, suddenly a Southern gentleman from the 1950s.

I laugh, then realize he's serious. "Really?"

"Really."

I pause, considering. But what is there to consider? Of course I want to go out with him. "Yeah. Okay."

"Then keep the jacket," he says, and I hug it closer.

I lean back against the door and he puts his palm on it, just over my shoulder. Now, he's fully aware he's doing the lean. And then he moves in to kiss me. He uses just the slightest hint of tongue this time, and I'm glad I'm not totally surprised by it. We stand there for a couple minutes, slowly saying good night, until the clock turns twelve. Then he heads off to his car.

When I go inside, I run up the stairs and lie there in my bed for a while, not able to fall asleep for the next two hours.

18. How to Make Tiramisu (And Not Eat It)

The next week is pretty much bliss. With Seth, at least. He walks me from class to class and holds my hand and corners me by the lockers and kisses me. Sometimes, I feel a little guilty when I see Taylor and her friends walk past. She notices. She still has that post-break-up glaze over her eyes, where everything about her is just a little sad. And it's not like it's been long at all since they broke up.

Her little posse shoots me wicked looks whenever they see me, which is kind of irritating, but also a little frightening. Taylor is nice enough, but I heard Ash once put bleach in a girl's mascara and sent her to the hospital. So I'm somewhat scared of the possible retribution they'll levy against me as soon as Taylor gets past the sad and into the anger.

But it's high school, and that kind of stuff happens, so I don't let the guilt overcome this walking-on-air feeling that follows me around everywhere. I keep instinctively pulling out my phone to text April about it, because I feel like I'm going to explode if I don't tell someone. But every time, I put it away. It's been too long since we've talked at this point, and I don't know if inching my way back in by bringing up Seth is the best idea ever. So, I hold it in. It's okay, because the giddiness overwhelms the almost-exploding-ness.

I practically skip into calculus, where April and I have been expertly avoiding each other for several days. She's sitting with Cash, fiddling with her lip ring. I feel a pang of longing at the familiar gesture, and my eyes start to sting. I miss her.

"Hey," I offer.

She rolls her eyes over to look at me and I shrink back in my seat. Then she raises her eyebrows and brings her palm to her chest. "Me?" she says, fluttering her eyelashes.

"Yeah. Hey."

"Ah, the prodigal daughter has returned," she says dramatically, so much bite in her voice I'm suddenly super glad she's sitting with Cash and not me.

"I just, uh."

She raises her eyebrows. "It's okay, sweetie. Sometimes it's hard to remember how to speak with the peasants once you've *ascended.*"

She shoots me an icy smile and I get this horrible hollow feeling in my stomach—one that slowly starts to take over everything, making all my limbs go hot, my face almost painfully so. "April, I'm, like . . . I'm sorry I've been blowing you off—"

She holds up a hand to cut me off. Cash just sits there uncomfortably.

"I don't care," she says.

I sink lower in my chair.

"I just need to know if you're going to debase your-self enough to come to math club tonight. Keith needs to know if he has to give you a ride."

"Well. I'm just, I'm not totally sure if—"

"Ugh, I hope he's incredible in bed," she says disgustedly.

I narrow my eyes. "Hey. That's not—"

But just then the bell rings and Mr. Sanchez looks pointedly at both of us and so we shut up. When class is over, she smiles brightly and waves that irritating, spirit fingers wave. I swear I'm not imagining when she leaves her middle finger up a little longer than the rest.

Everything else sucks for the whole day. I'm being totally antisocial, unable to focus on anything but April and how desperately I do not want to bump into her.

Finally, miracle of miracles, cooking rolls around (never thought I'd say those words), and I practically fall into the lockers next to Seth. He takes my hand, rubbing his thumb over it. "You want to come over tonight?"

I feel a flood of relief (and hormones) and all the April crap flies out of my head. "Maybe."

He grins. "My parents aren't home."

My heart starts thumping; I'm not exactly sure what that implies. "Um."

"That doesn't mean 'Come over and sleep with me,' by the way. It means 'Come over and I'll make you tiramisu and maybe make out with you on the couch.'"

I laugh, releasing the nervous tension that built up faster than I thought nervous tension could build in a person. "In that case, yes, I'm totally free."

"Good. Do I need to pick you up? I can, but you'll have to wait longer for dessert."

"No, it's fine. I can just borrow my dad's car."

The bell rings, signaling we have three minutes until class starts.

"Your dad lets you drive his car?" Seth asks.

"There's basically nothing my dad doesn't let me do."

"Lucky."

Seth loosens his grip on my fingers for just a second, and at that moment, I turn around and see Drew coming down the hallway. I snatch my hand back from Seth's instinctively and he frowns at me. But Drew doesn't see a thing. I don't know why it matters. It doesn't. But the fact that I've been dating Seth for over a week and Drew still (to my knowledge) doesn't have any idea feels like a good thing.

I ignore the weird look on Seth's face, and when the bell rings, we head to class and neither of us says a word about it.

♉

Later that night, after my makeup is done in a way that took an hour but looks like it took five minutes, I sit at my computer. Ever since I wrote "How to Make Out," my blog views have gone from high to insanely high. With that, so has my PayPal account. I'm almost halfway to what I need for New York. So obviously, my inbox is inundated with questions in that vein—questions I'm eager to answer even though they make me kind of uncomfortable. The thing is, I want New York. I *really* want April to stop being pissed at me for blowing her off that night (though, admittedly, she's probably angrier that I haven't really tried to talk to her since), and working this hard for the trip might force her into some level of forgiveness. And answering something stupid is probably the way to get that money.

How do I give . . . Whoa, yeah, not that one. I don't care how much you paid me.

How do I hold hands right? That will earn me nothing.

And then, the moneymaker: *How do I get rid of a hickey?*

I take a deep breath and make my decision. Then I go downstairs.

"Hey, Dad, can I borrow your car?"

He's sitting on the couch with Stacey, watching some sappy movie he would never have agreed to watch with Mom. But he looks up from what I'm sure is a captivating scene and answers, "What do you need it for?"

"I'm going to Seth's."

He reaches into his pocket and throws me the keys without another word. No "Make good decisions, sweetie," or "Be home by eleven." If I were going somewhere with Drew, he would have held on to those keys like his fingers were in rigor mortis. But with Seth, it's easy. Nice change of pace.

I leave, not even obligated to acknowledge Stacey since she's so sucked into her movie, and speed all the way over to Seth's.

When I get there, I notice the conspicuous lack of cars in his driveway, which solidifies the "parents not home" claim, and twists a knot in my stomach. It feels a little prostitute-esque, getting a boy to give me a hickey for a blog answer people will pay me for. Maybe I am kind of a hooker, committing semi-sexual acts for money. I almost wish his parents were here, so I would have to reconsider. But they're not, and I'm not going back on this now. Besides, I like him. So it's not exactly the same.

I walk up to the door and knock, and when he opens it for me, the smells wafting out from the kitchen are like paradise. Coffee and cream and cake and basically everything that adds girth to your hips but is so worth it, you don't care.

"Hey," he says, kissing me chastely on the cheek.

"It smells crazy amazing in here."

"Just wait till you taste it. Have you ever had tiramisu?"

"I've had tiramisu-flavored ice cream."

He shakes his head and clucks his tongue. "So much to teach you."

I smile and head into the kitchen. "Anything I can help with?"

"Nope. Not tonight. Tonight I'm cooking *for* you, no lesson required."

"So, how long until I can try this allegedly mind-blowing dessert?"

He grabs my hand. Seth, I have learned, is extremely into hand-holding, which is completely cool with me. We're heading into this little room off the kitchen. It's already dark and the TV is on, but it's muted.

"We just have to wait a little while for it to cool."

"Okay," I say, and when we sit on the couch, the only light glowing in from the kitchen and the TV, I start fidgeting. Maybe I shouldn't do this. Maybe this is crossing a line. No. I'm doing it. Maybe not yet. I don't know.

"Let's play a game," I blurt out.

"What kind of game?"

"Two Truths and a Lie."

He scoots a little closer to me. "I've never played."

I cluck my tongue and grin. "So many things to teach you."

He laughs.

"So the game goes like this. I'll tell you three things about me. Two of them are true. One isn't. And it's your job to guess which is the lie."

"What happens if I guess right?"

"Huh. I don't know. I owe you a kiss, maybe."

"That seems fair."

"I'll go first, so you can't blame losing on not knowing the rules. I don't have a license, I'm a sophomore, and my favorite color is purple."

"Okay, I know you're a sophomore. I've never seen you drive or wear the color purple. I'm going with . . . oh no, wait. You drove here tonight. You have a license."

"Correct, sir. I owe you a kiss."

"You do indeed."

I lean forward and kiss him, not lingering. It's the first question of the game, after all.

"My turn. I play pool. I'm terrible at math AND science. And I'm a virgin."

"Ooh. It just got interesting. You do suck at math, and I'm going to guess science goes along with that. And you seem like the kind of guy who plays pool. I bet you have a table in your basement. I do not believe, however, that you're a virgin, not after the length of time you dated Taylor Krissick."

"Wrong."

"Liar."

"I do not cheat at these games. We never went all the way. I'm amazing at biology, though."

"So now what? I got the answer wrong."

"I think that means you owe me another kiss."

I grin. "Fair enough. Where?"

He raises an eyebrow and points to his mouth. Not creative, but I can work with it. I grab his collar and pull him toward me and kiss him, long and slow. When he pulls back, I scoot closer to him.

"My turn. I'm deathly afraid of spiders. I've only *really* kissed two guys ever, yourself included, and I speak fluent French."

"You hustled me, Renley Eisler. Baited me with easy questions. And now here we are. I'm going with French. You don't speak French."

"Au contraire, monsieur. I speak French like a native. I did have a pet spider until he died two years ago."

"And the guys? Who else did you kiss?"

"That's not part of the rules."

"Fair enough."

"So, you lost. Which means you owe *me* a kiss."

He moves close. "Where?" He expects me to say the lips. I almost want to. But I also want to authentically answer that question. So I trail my finger down to a point just below my ear. He follows my finger with his eyes and then stares at me for a second, but he moves forward then and kisses me, right where my finger used to be, edge of his lips just grazing my ear. Something about that spot sends shivers down my spine, and I wish he'd kiss me more than once. He lingers, then pulls back.

"Now me. My name is Seth Levine. I'm a senior. And I don't want to stop playing this game and kiss you right now, more than once, more than for a second."

The corners of my mouth turn up in a ghost of a smile and he leans in, kissing me deeper than he ever has. And from my limited experience, he's good at it. His fingers press into my back and in my hair, kiss strong and unyielding and exhilarating. And then, like I figured he'd do, he trails his mouth over to my ear and down my neck.

I lean back against the couch, turning my neck toward him, blog barely registering in the back of my mind. He kisses my throat and then back up to my jaw, and my nerves are completely on fire. I can feel his teeth when he bites down just a little, not enough to really hurt, just enough to send those delicious chills everywhere at once.

We both completely forget about the tiramisu cooling in the fridge.

19. HOW to cover a Hickey

The next morning is Sunday. I sleep in way too long. When I finally force myself to get up, I check in the mirror, and, sure enough, there's a little purple mark just below my jaw. It's far enough back that my hair could cover it if it had to, but that's not quite enough material to post on. So I head to the kitchen.

The frozen spoon does nothing but make my neck cold. Though on second thought, it might make the color go down a little. I try massaging it to get the blood flowing there again, and that really does nothing. So I try running a hairbrush over it (which hurts and makes it worse), but after a few minutes, it starts to go down, and then I try the spoon again. Not too shabby.

Several combinations of makeup later, and I'm writing a post.

A few minutes after I hit PUBLISH, my phone buzzes.

Hey stranger.

Hey

Come over. It's been a hundred years since you came over.

I smile—I see him like every day when he gives me rides, but it's been a while since we just hung out. I shut the phone, not bothering to text back. I'll be at Drew's within a couple minutes anyway.

I knock on his window and he slides it open. Expert Ms. Calloway avoidance.

"I've missed you," he says, wrapping me up in a hug.

"You too."

He sits back on his bed and I sit beside him. Despite the fact that the last time we saw each other was . . . tense, to say the least, it doesn't feel weird to me anymore. And Drew seems totally normal. He flips on the TV and we just hang out wordlessly until a commercial comes on.

"So," he says, smirking, "'How to Get Rid of a Hickey,' huh?"

Everything on me flashes hot. "What?"

"I don't remember even kissing your neck. Did I?" From the corner of my eye, I can see him grinning deviously.

"No," I say, voice quiet.

"Ah, so you're fibbing on the blog now, oh certified expert."

It feels like a long time before I finally answer, "No."

He glances over at me, then flicks his gaze down to my jaw. His face falls immediately. "Oh."

And then nothing. This overwhelming sense of guilt floods over me, which is totally ridiculous. I didn't do anything wrong.

"It's Seth, isn't it?" he says, voice so quiet I can barely hear him over the TV, which wasn't loud to begin with.

I don't look at him. "Yes."

"You guys together now?"

"Yeah."

"For how long?"

I sigh. "About a week and a half."

He's quiet. Really quiet.

"I should have told you earlier," I say.

"No, it's fine. You don't owe me an explanation. It's not like our little make out session in the woods meant anything." There's not a hint of sarcasm in his voice, which makes it way worse.

"Come on, Drew."

"Seriously. You don't have to tell me about all your romantic conquests. It's fine. I don't tell you about all of mine."

"Okay," I say, beginning to wish I hadn't come over.

"I did have this girl a few weeks ago, though. Amazing. Like, seriously amazing. I almost invited her over for round two. But, you know, policy."

I'm totally silent, frowning deep.

"And you call that a hickey?" he continues. "You should have seen the marks I left on this girl. And a lot more places than just her jaw."

My pulse jumps and I can feel my fists clench at my sides.

"Not that that's a totally unprecedented event. Before that—"

"Drew!" I say.

He turns over to look at me, almost sneering. I've never seen a look like this on his face. Ever.

"What?"

"Stop."

"What? You jealous?"

I get up out of the bed, stiff and shaking everywhere, instantly angry.

"You're just being an idiot. Why would I want to hear about all the places you've bitten girls and all the different sexual partners you've had in the last month?"

"If you're not jealous, why do you care?"

"Because it's disgusting," I shout, shaking harder now.

"Well maybe I don't want a detailed description of how some douchebag guy you're dating sucked on your neck for three hours."

"Then stop reading my blog, stalker."

"Maybe you should stop whoring yourself out for your precious readers, and it wouldn't matter what I read."

I recoil and shake my head, hard. A huge vein pulses in his neck and his eyes are cold and hard. "Why are you being like this?"

"*Because*, Renley, I . . ." he trails off and leans back against his headboard. "I can't do this right now. I have my own shit to deal with, and I can't add you to it all."

"What is that supposed to mean?"

"It means I need a break from this twisted, screwed up relationship."

I step backward. It feels like someone just knocked the wind out of me. "What?"

"You just . . . after the other day, it's not the same. I can't do this. Be with you all the time, wanting to kiss you, knowing what it feels like to kiss you. Wanting to touch you and knowing what that feels like, too. It's screwed up."

"So you're what? Ending everything?"

"No. I can't do that either. I just know that this"—he points back and forth between us— "isn't normal. And it's not something I can honestly handle, not with you jerking me around and then getting hickeys and who knows what else from some other guy. I'm not pissed, I'm . . . I'll be fine. We'll be fine. I just . . ." He looks totally tortured, which would make me feel worse if he weren't about to thrust what feels like shards of glass into my heart. "I just need you to leave me alone for a while."

I blink rapidly and bite down and suck hard on my tongue. I heard once that if you do that, it's impossible to cry. And I won't cry. Not right now. Not in front of him, this way. So I stumble out, out of his window, and say, "Okay. Bye." And I turn around and run all the way back home, because if I don't, I'll lose it right there in his bedroom.

This sucks. This whole thing sucks. I can't think about it. But I can't not. This is not fair in the slightest. What gives him the right to decide who I can date? Who I can kiss? Who can give me hickeys wherever and whenever I want them to? I can't stand this, and I'm about to actually hyperventilate.

Without really thinking, I pull out my phone and send a text to Mom. I don't think about when she'll answer, or if she will. I just do it.

Mom I really really need to talk to you. I'm having the worst day.

And SEND.

Seconds later, it's marked as delivered. She hasn't read it yet.

And now I'm back in panic mode, knowing she won't respond and neither would Drew and April hates me and Seth wouldn't understand.

There's a knock on my door, and I don't tell whoever it is to come in, because if I do, I'll make it as far as "Co—" and then I'll explode.

My dad cracks the door open anyway and I crawl into my bed, pulling the covers up to my chin. "Honey?" he says.

Apparently hearing someone else speak was enough to open the floodgates. I break into giant, gasping sobs, and he freezes.

"Leelee, what's wrong? Something with your big trip?" He rushes over to the bed and I just shake my head and throw my arms around his neck. His shirt is drenched within thirty seconds. I grab a hold of him tightly and he hugs me back, strong arms anchoring me there, letting me freak out. Eventually, I'm able to calm down.

"What's wrong?" he whispers, chin atop my head.

"I can't," I say in hiccupping little syllables.

"You can tell me anything."

"I want to talk to Mom."

He's quiet for a while. "Do you want me to send Stacey?"

I shake my head hard. "I think . . . I think I just need to sit here for a while."

He doesn't break the hug for a good long time, which is okay with me. But after a while, he leaves, and he turns off the light. It's midafternoon, but I curl up on my side and, without meaning to, without knowing I'm doing it at all, I fall asleep.

It's dark when I wake up, and I can feel the cold air sighing in through the window I never closed. The thing that sucks is I don't feel any better.

There's one message on my phone, and I reach for it hesitantly. My pulse jumps. It's from Mom.

Sry u r having a bad day. Sux. Am out w/ hubs + daughter. Talk 2 u l8er? Xoxoxo

And like a whole line of emojis.

I throw the phone down. She won't call me later. All I am is a reminder of what she used to have, and of what Dad and Stacey did to her. She has another cuter, less painful three-year-old daughter with her "hubs" and if that's enough for her, fine.

But damn, I wish I could talk to her. I can't. And honestly, that hurts worse than Drew.

I want to be able to talk to her about the cute guy who likes me and who kissed me and asked me out and cooked for me. And I want to tell her about April, and how I think it's ridiculous that we're still fighting somehow over nothing. And I want to talk about Drew and have her tell me that it'll be fine and that he's being unfair and stupid and that he'll come back around eventually. I'd like her to be ticked because she can see my hickey through my makeup. But she's not.

Suddenly, the room feels tiny and suffocating, and I need to be outside. So I clamber out onto my window-sill and grab the roofline, hoisting myself up. I'm wearing a tank top and miniscule boxers, and it's freezing, and the shingles are rough against my legs, but I like it that way. I look around quickly, and I don't see anyone, so I let myself think about her. Let it all overwhelm me. And then, the flood.

I'm crying so hard I can't even see through the tears, can barely breathe. There's a horrible pain in my chest, a hollow. It almost hurts to cry this hard. I'm so wrapped up in everything, so solitary in this moment, that I can't even hear when he crosses his yard to mine.

"Renley?" he calls, and I do hear that.

I stop crying for a second and manage, "What?"

He hops up onto my windowsill. "Can I come up?"

I scowl and whip my head around to face him. "Are you *kidding me?*"

But I don't say no, and we both know it. So he climbs up next to me.

"Are you okay?"

I'm doing that post-weeping gasping thing when I answer, "No."

"Is this because of me? Because I'm really sorry about the 'whoring yourself out for your readers' thing. That was shitty. And I didn't mean that we're done forever. I just meant—"

"Not everything I feel is always because of you, Drew," I spit. He doesn't say anything. I let myself breathe for a second, and eventually sigh "No."

He inches closer to me. "Then what is it?"

I make myself forget that just hours ago he was banishing me from his life, and I pretend that everything is normal. Otherwise, I have no one to talk to, and I can't deal with that right now. "It's stupid."

"Try me."

"I just . . ." When I start to form the words, I can feel a bubble in the back of my throat, strangling me. "I just miss my mom." And I lose it again.

He wraps his arms around my shoulders, pulling me in tight to his chest. "You're killing me, R," he whispers.

"You shouldn't be up here with me. We're taking a break." My words are muffled in his jacket.

"Not tonight. I'm not leaving you like this."

"You have to."

"No I don't. You're coming over."

I raise up my head a fraction. "I can't. Not after—"

"Forget what I said. We'll remember that tomorrow."

"And I can't spend the night. I have a boyfriend."

"Screw your boyfriend. Think about him tomorrow too. Tonight, you need to come with me. I don't care what I said. I'm not leaving you, not like this. And you'd better come to my house, because the alternative is for us to stay out on this roof all night, and I'm not giving you my jacket. Why don't you ever remember to wear a jacket?"

I smile a little despite myself and let him pull me up. Then we slide off the roof to the windowsill to the ground. I walk with him to his room.

"What were you doing outside anyway?" I ask, tears gone for a moment.

"Mom's usual."

I nod and climb in his window after him. We can both hear his mom hooking up with someone in the background.

He strips off his jacket and his shirt and jeans, down to his boxers. It feels strange this time, but I don't say anything about it.

"Come on," he says, nodding toward the bed.

I slip in beside him and lay my head on his chest, craving the familiar comfort of his arm, his heartbeat beneath my ear.

"It's never stupid to miss her," he says, his voice vibrating in my ear.

I can feel a cry rising up in my throat.

"I miss my dad every day. He left when I was seven. Seven. You remember?" I nod into his chest. Of course I remember. "I still think about him. I wonder if he's off in another country, doing spy work like my mom used to tell me. Or if he's getting drunk somewhere where everybody knows him. If he's fishing with some other kid in some other family he picked. What a pussy, right? Ten years, and I'm still not over it." His voice cracks.

I lie still there for a while, then say softly, "My mom left five years ago. I was eleven."

"Yeah," he says.

That was when I kissed Drew for the first time. Out by the creek, before I told him what had happened.

I sniff. "I thought we had a good thing, you know? Regular mom-daughter stuff. Hair and dress-up and ballet recitals and stupid weepy chick flicks. But when my dad cheated, she just left. All of us. She left *me*. How do you leave your kid over a *guy*? She doesn't even call me, Drew. I used to call all the time, but now even if I do, she's free for five minutes and then she leaves, or usually, she doesn't even answer. She never texts. She didn't send me a card for my birthday. My sixteenth birthday. Nothing. She might as well be freaking dead." I pause. Then, "What am I supposed to do without my mom?"

He hugs me so close to his chest, I can hardly breathe. But it feels safe. It feels like the only thing keeping me from coming apart at the seams. We lie there like that for so long, I know he must be sleeping. But then I hear him say, "It wasn't you, R."

I don't say anything; I just look up at him.

"Your mom left because of your mom. Not because of you."

"How do you know?" I ask weakly.

"Because anyone who has you all to themselves and leaves is insane."

I relax into him. "I'm sorry about your dad."

He breathes deeply in and out. "I'm sorry about all of this."

"I'm sorry you had to hear me cry and ruin all your plans to stay away from me."

"Tomorrow," he says. "Tomorrow, I'll get up before you do, and I'll leave. And you can go back home and not text me for a while. And you'll be okay and I'll be okay. And you can go back to having an amazing boyfriend and smiling and being happy-go-lucky Renley. But none of that matters today. Okay?"

"Okay."

I can feel the sad smile in his voice when he says, "This is so messed up."

And I smile into his chest in that same broken way. And fall asleep.

20. How to Get Someone Else a Black Eye

I wake up early, but he's gone, like he said he'd be. It doesn't hurt this morning—I think because I knew it was coming. And maybe because I know he doesn't hate me, not really. So when I swing my legs over the side of his bed, I feel okay. And when I show up at the bus stop for the first time in I don't know how long, it sucks, but I'm not dead. I'm not even really numb. I'm just . . . okay.

I head to the back of the bus and slink into the seat, sliding low and shoving my headphones in my ears. Freshmen. So many tiny freshmen everywhere doing freshmen things. I stare out the window, vision cut off by the line of the window. And no matter how loud I turn my iPod, everyone else on the bus manages to overwhelm the music. That's it. I am not doing this tomorrow.

Hey

Hey :) Seth texts.

So, you would LOVE to give me a ride to school tomorrow right?

I must live even closer to the school than I remember, because before Seth can even text me back, the behemoth of a vehicle groans to a slow stop.

I don't get up for a couple minutes. No sense in doing that; the horde of kids in front of me will take a millennium to vacate the bus. My phone buzzes.

Banished to the bus this morning?

Ugh.

I'll meet you there

When the majority of the students have finally flooded out into the courtyard, I stand and stick my phone in my pocket, then burst forth from the mobile prison. Ah, freedom and fresh air absent of body odor.

I descend the little half-steps down onto the sidewalk and find Seth there, smiling at me. He holds his hand out and I take it, intertwining his fingers with mine. He leans over and kisses me on the cheek.

"So, you need a ride tomorrow?"

"Tomorrow. Possibly the day after. The time period is indeterminate."

"I can do that."

"Good. What's the use of having a boyfriend who can drive if you can't take advantage of his license?"

He knocks his fist to his heart, faking shock and horror. "You would use me in such a way? I'm appalled."

I shrug. "I'm just terrible and awful. What can I say?"

He moves his fingers just a little over mine, giving me a rush. "So I'll pick you up tomorrow morning, and indefinitely ever after. Out of curiosity, what caused this sudden change in transportation plans?"

"Oh, my ride just kind of bailed on me."

"Who?" His tone is nonchalant; he's not asking in a jealous way, I know. But it makes me uncomfortable to answer.

"Uh, Drew."

He stops short and turns to face me. "Drew? Drew Calloway has been your ride to school this whole time?" he says, voice sharp.

"Yes. I did say I was sleeping with Drew Calloway this whole time. Oh no, wait. Yeah, still just my ride to school."

He purses his lips. "I'm sorry. It's fine. I just didn't know you were getting rides with *him* every day."

Something about the way he says *him* makes me bristle. "You knew we were friends."

"Yeah. I did. I'm sorry; it's not a big thing. I hear that name, I automatically assume any girl associated with him is someone he's seeing naked. Reflex."

My grip on his hand relaxes a little, and we make our way closer to the school. I stop with him and lean up against the cold brick.

"I don't know what I'm getting jealous about anyway." He brings my hand up and fiddles with my fingers. "Drew Calloway doesn't get to do this."

175

"True," I say, blood flowing up to my cheeks.

"And he doesn't get to do this." He kisses me right below my ear. I shiver. Then he moves over to my mouth and kisses me slowly, parting my lips and running his fingers over my jaw. "And Drew has never kissed you." He smiles and I flush, partly from the heat of the kiss, partly because that is not strictly true.

When I don't say anything, he twitches his head a fraction of an inch. "Drew has never kissed you, I said."

"Yeah, I heard."

He backs up. "Has he?"

I roll my eyes. "What do you care?"

"Because you told me you guys were friends."

"We are."

"Is that a service you provide all your friends?"

I narrow my eyes and slide out and away from the brick.

"Was it just like, once?"

"No." I have my back turned to him when I answer, power-walking to the front door.

"When?"

"Like three weeks ago, Seth. You and I weren't dating, if that's what you're wondering."

"Three weeks?" His voice goes all high and weird. "And not just once. And you've been getting rides to school from him every day, even since we've been dating, and you haven't even told me?"

I stop short and turn around, arms folded tight across my chest, high ponytail whipping across my face. "It doesn't *matter*. There was nothing to tell. And seriously, possessive is not an attractive look on you."

"I wouldn't be being possessive if your 'best friend' whom you occasionally kiss, apparently, wasn't the biggest man whore in school."

I never thought I'd say I wanted to slap Seth Levine across his pretty face. But I want to slap Seth Levine across his pretty face.

I back away a couple steps, hands up, shaking my head. "I do not even know what to say to that. Forget the ride to school tomorrow."

Then I stomp off, brand-new high heels clacking on the pavement.

"Wait," he says, but I'm already in the hallway, and within minutes, I'm slamming my butt down on my chair in math class and huffing a shrill, angry-cheerleader huff.

"Whoa. You look like someone just, I don't know, punted your dog."

"What?" I say, turning to April. I'm basically floored that she's talking to me at all. That dry sarcasm is still an undercurrent in her voice, but the acid isn't quite so close to the surface.

"I mean, you don't look like they killed your dog, per se. Just insulted it."

"Uh . . ."

"What?" she asks. "Trouble in paradise?"

She sighs, gives me a once-over, and finally rolls her eyes and moves over a couple desks, sitting next to me.

"It's Seth. And Drew. And . . . we have two minutes till class starts and I have many words to say."

She pauses and fiddles with her lip ring. I wonder if she sees the hope in my eyes. I bet I look like a total plastic, face bright and eager. Overeager, like if we don't fix this thing, I'll deflate and die.

"Free after school?" she says, not quite smiling, but not scowling either.

I'm not sure how much my face reflects it, but I'm definitely feeling the April-shaped chasm in my chest. Even if I weren't free after school today, well, I would be.

"Totally."

Her face brightens a little the same time mine does, and then the bell rings. And the ever-scintillating lecture begins.

After class, Seth is waiting for me at the door, avoiding my eyes. April shoots me a knowing look and darts off, black and blue hair bouncing on her shoulders. It feels sudden, but awesome, April not totally hating me. But it feels not-awesome to have Seth looking like that.

"Can I talk to you?" he asks, and his eyes are big and round and sad.

"Sure. I have a free period."

He nods. "I have gym. Who cares about gym?"

He hesitates, then slides his fingers down the inside of my arm to take my hand, and I let him, trying to ignore the chills I get from the light touch.

We walk together like that to his car and I get in.

"Where are we going?" I ask, stomach aflutter, cold and hollow.

"Park?"

"Okay." There's a little park just down the road from here. It's always empty on weekdays, except for the ducks, and even they aren't there during the winter. At night, kids go there sometimes to make out (or finalize illicit drug deals, depending).

The trip is pretty quiet, but he never takes his hand off mine, which keeps my heart rate normal. If I thought I'd screwed things up with this guy after a week and a half, I'd be a mess right now.

He parks and we head down the little cement walking path to the slushy pond and sit.

"I'm sorry," he says.

"Okay."

"I just know you and Drew have always been just this side of an item, and I'd hate to be caught in the middle of something. Especially when I don't know about it."

"And you're getting all this because I kissed him once? Well. More than once."

"Three weeks ago."

"Yeah, I see what you're saying." I turn toward him. "Look," I say, "he's my best friend. And he's been in love with me for, like, ever. And I slipped and we made out and that's it. And then you and I started dating and I forgot all about it. End of story."

Seth is quiet for a while. "So there's nothing going on then?"

"No. Absolutely not."

"Is he still in love with you?"

I sigh. "Yes."

"You sure?"

"We talked about it, like, two days ago."

He turns his head sharply and raises his eyebrows. "Seriously?"

"Don't worry about it."

His face darkens considerably and he tosses a rock into the lake.

I sigh dramatically. "Really, Seth. We have an hour plus lunch. Do you think I really wanted to come here and talk about some other guy and be angsty for my whole free period?"

He looks over at me and grins. "You're right. It would be a real waste of ninety minutes."

I'm glad we're alone, because even if he's kind of stupid, I really just want to kiss him for the next, well, however long we feel like. And so I do.

Ꮥ

After cooking lets out, Seth and I part ways, and I text April, finalizing our plans for later. I wander around the halls for a little while, trying to decide how to get home. It's cold and I've already missed the bus. Maybe I could find Seth and hitch a ride.

I turn aimlessly for a while until I hear voices murmuring. One of them sounds like Seth's. The other one, for sure, is Drew's. I peek around the corner into a hallway. A couple kids are standing around, but beyond that it's mostly empty. From where I'm standing, I can hear Seth saying, "Listen, I'm not trying to start anything."

"Okay," Drew says coolly.

"I'm just asking you, man to man, if you could cool it with Renley. She's my girlfriend, okay?"

Drew leans back against the wall, hands in his pockets. "Cool what with Renley?"

Seth gives him a look. "I know you care about her. I just need you to be cool. Can you do that?"

"What, she told you about last night?"

Oh no. Not last night. I'm going to die. I'm actually going to die. Should I stop it? No, then they'll know I've been eavesdropping. And even if they don't, I'm going to have to explain *something* to Seth about last night now.

Seth cocks his head. "Last night?"

Drew gets up from the wall and calmly says, "Last night was nothing. She needed a friend. I'm convenient. So I let her stay with me."

"What?" Seth says, his voice dangerously quiet.

"Like I said, nothing happened. I'm not gonna sleep with another guy's girlfriend."

"She stayed all night with you? Did she sleep in your bed?"

Drew rolls his eyes. "Yes. But I'm telling you, nothing—"

Seth steps forward and pushes him. This is not good. Stop, Seth. I'm dating the guy, so I should honestly be idealizing his capability to beat every other male into a pulp, but even I know he doesn't stand a chance against Drew.

Drew freezes. "Don't."

"You slept with my girlfriend in your bed, and you want me to stop?" He pushes him again.

Drew hardly twitches. If anything, his stance is firmer. I can see his fist curling at his side.

"Listen, man. I actually like you. So don't *touch* me again, 'cause I really don't want to hurt you."

Seth's lips pull back into an almost snarl. "You don't want me to touch you? Then don't touch my girlfriend, dick."

Drew's jaw clenches and his eyes spark. I've seen this look before. I can tell what's coming, but I'm frozen in place.

"Settle down there, Cro Magnon. Defending your woman's honor or whatever it is you're trying to do. She's been your girlfriend for about two minutes. She's been sleeping in my bed for two *years*."

Seth pulls his arm back and throws a punch. And just as I figured, Drew sidesteps it with very little effort, so Seth's fist pounds against the wall. Drew shakes his head and straightens, rolling his shoulders, and when Seth rebounds from the wall, Drew swings. Hard.

His fist slams into Seth's face with a thud and Seth falls. Drew shakes his head again and walks down the hall without looking back. When he sees me, he doesn't slow down. He just quietly says, "Sorry about your boyfriend's face."

My mouth is hanging open like a cartoon's. And I can't face Seth right now. I don't even want him to know I saw. So I tuck tail and turn. I'll walk home.

21. HOW to Fix a Broken Thing

Hey April. What if I just came and picked you up in my dad's car right now? Would that be cool?

Sure. See you in a few

I snatch the keys from their hook and shut the front door behind me, then barrel down the road to April's house. I choose to ignore the dread pooling in my stomach over seeing Seth, whenever I do inevitably have to see him, and just let myself be happy to see April. It's silly to be this excited over seeing her, probably. But it's been *how* long since I hung out with another girl who was not Stacey?

When I pull in her driveway, she's sitting by the window. She notices I'm there, and my palms go all sweaty and shaky. I roll my eyes at myself. What am I so nervous about? It's not like I'm planning to lose my virginity to her tonight or something.

She hops in the car and smiles hugely, which somehow makes me more nervous.

"So. Where are we going?"

I wiggle my fingers at her.

"Manicures?" she guesses.

"I think that's the best course of action," I say.

She stares down at her cuticles and sighs heavily. "Yes, my winter hands are out of control."

Then there's a silence that stretches on for the longest sixty seconds that have ever existed. My heart starts to flutter, and I can finally pinpoint the crappy feeling in my stomach, the lead ball that's taken up residence since I picked up April. Guilt.

I can't stop thinking that she's going to just up and start yelling at me before we get to the mall, like she did back in class. I don't even think I can be a great participant in any conversation, because I'm just waiting for her to bring up the party and the total phone silence for . . . when was the last time we even talked?

So, I'm sitting there, silently ticking the minutes away, hoping she doesn't bring up anything. When she doesn't, of course, I bring it up.

"I'm really sorry about—"

"So, the last couple weeks—"

We stop and look at each other for a second.

"You first," she says. Oh great. Thanks for that.

I keep my eyes on the road. This is partially because, well, I'm driving. But more so because it's awkward. "I'm sorry about the whole party thing. It was really crappy of me." I take another deep breath, knuckles white on the steering wheel. "And I'm sorry I haven't tried to call you or text you or anything since."

"To be fair, I could have called you."

"Yeah, but I was the one who did the stupid thing to begin with. Kind of my job to make first contact, isn't it?"

"Yeah, you're right. This was totally your fault; I was just trying to be nice."

"Hey!" I say, hitting her on the shoulder. She laughs and I break into an easy smile and turn up the radio.

When we get to the mall, April literally leaps from the vehicle and grabs my hand, moving toward the building at such a rapid pace, I'm totally stumbling across the parking lot. The random spots of ice here and there do not help the situation.

She lets go of my hand and bursts into the mall, energy radiating from everywhere around her. I, unfortunately, fall into said doors from the sheer momentum. But it's cool. She's excited, I'm excited, and a door and nose are both slightly worse for the wear. Things could be worse.

We walk together down the tile halls, occasionally bombarded by the smells of Starbucks or cookie pizzas or enormous amounts of leather wafting out from Brookstone. But, after passing store after store and avoiding one person with a European accent and unbelievable smile trying to wrangle us into buying $150 curling irons, I detect the familiar scent of acetone.

We both prance in and the lady at the front raises her eyebrows a little when she sees April. Admittedly, the giant turquoise outline of her hair is eyebrow-raise-worthy. April either doesn't notice or doesn't care.

"Do you guys have time for two walk-ins?" she asks.

"What service?"

"We," she says, grabbing my shoulder, "are in desperate need of manicures."

"Tips or polish?"

I go for tips. April, to the surprise of no one in the room, heads straight for the neon polish shades, twisting her lip ring as she considers. After much deliberation, she raises a bottle of lime green and smiles triumphantly.

"Can I get tips in this?"

The lady raises an eyebrow again. If she doesn't like the color, I don't know why she stocks it. Either way, she nods, and April and I go over to the chairs and sit. A girl and a guy emerge from somewhere in the back, and the older, judgy lady sits back at the front desk. I am not disappointed.

The guy sits in front of me, and the girl in front of April. She has a pink streak running through her hair, and her nails are painted with this crackle stuff that was big in the nineties, and again a year or so ago, but not so much now. She's perfect for April.

The guy picks up both of my hands and smiles. "Beautiful hands," he says. He winks, and I blush. Then they go to work.

"So," April says, "tell me about your boy drama."

I groan. "It's just . . . a lot of ridiculousness. Seth and I are together now, you know."

She stiffens barely, almost imperceptibly, but I see it. "Yeah, I figured when I saw you guys holding hands and sucking each other's tongues off in the halls."

"Yeah. Well. Anyway. He's pissed at me now because he found out Drew and I kissed—"

"Wait. What? You kissed Drew? When? Where? Oh my gosh, how did I not know this?" Her eyes widen, and I think some of the excited surprise there is genuine, but mixed in with that is a thread of hurt, betrayal. How did I not tell her right after?

I grin anyway, pretending along with her that there's not this awkward ribbon of hurt between us. "Yeah, we kissed."

"That's *it*? No. That is a terrible story. I do not accept your offering. When?"

"A few weeks ago."

"Was it just, like, a 'My aunt kisses me like this when she leaves after Thanksgiving' kiss? Or a world-rocking, feel it all the way down to your toes kind of kiss?"

Now I'm thinking about it all and my skin is prickling. I can feel the blood rushing to my cheeks.

April grins deviously. "I knew it. I knew you guys would hook up eventually."

I can see the girl working on April's nails stifle a giggle.

"We didn't hook up. We kissed. That's it. Well, not totally it. But anyway—"

"That's not it? What else? You're obligated to tell me. It's in the best friend contract."

I look around the room and lean into April's ear and whisper it. "We made out in the woods. And it was good. Unbelievably good. And he . . ." I sigh, embarrassed to even be talking about this, just because it's never been me saying these things. To anyone. Ever. "Let's just say I was half-naked by the end of it. And so was he."

She snaps her face toward me, eyes huge. "Which half?"

"April!" I hiss. Then I roll my eyes. "The top half."

"No bra even?" She's talking mostly low, but she is definitely *not* making as much of an effort as me to be quiet. I swear the woman at the front is about to throw nail polish remover all over her.

I lower my voice even more. "No. No bra."

"Renley, Renley. What has happened to you in the last few weeks? My little baby's growing up."

"Ugh, shut up. Anyway, so I wasn't cheating on Seth or anything. But Seth found out about it, and he got all pissed off for some reason."

April scoffs. 'Cause yeah, he was being totally ridiculous.

"So we talked it out, kissed it out, and I thought we were good. But then after school, I walked by the science hall and there's Drew and Seth talking. Not in a friendly way. So Drew let it slip that I spent the night at his house last night—"At that, April balks again, but I push on through."—and Seth tried to hit him."

"Bad call," April says.

"Yeah. Drew knocked him to the ground with one punch."

"Well, obviously."

"I know. I didn't even go help him up or anything. I can't face him now. What am I going to say? 'Hey, love. I was telling the truth. Nothing's going on with Drew. Also we kissed and I spent the night in his bed last night, and

Drew was in his underwear. We're just friends. How do you not get that?'"

April laughs. "Yeah, what was that about? I mean, I know you spend the night over there all the time, but you do have a boyfriend. That's kind of not cool."

My shoulders fall. "I know. And seriously, nothing happened. I was just having a really hard time last night and it's not like I could come talk to you. So I talked to Drew, and I fell asleep."

That stiffness is back in her again, but she covers it with a pseudo-sympathetic smile. "Well, Seth will get over it. And if he doesn't, screw that."

"Yeah." I lean my head back against the chair as the manicurist starts applying the tips. "Hey, we haven't even talked about you. What's going on in your life?"

She bites her lip and says, "Oh, nothing really."

"Lie."

"Nothing. Cash and I are still going out. Still saving up for NYC. That's it."

"How's your brother?"

She looks away from me. "Fine."

"And?"

She makes an exasperated noise and looks back at my face. "He's . . . well, he's decided to join the army. Just like I knew he would."

I'm not sure what to say. "Did . . . when does he go?"

"He heads to basic in December. And now he's spending all this time with all his stupid friends and he's just totally ignoring me. I don't even care."

I don't believe that for a second. Tears well up in her eyes, threatening to spill over. I jiggle my leg nervously. When April cries, I just have no idea how I'm supposed to handle it. I don't think giving her a hug is appropriate. I mean, especially not right now—my hands are kind of occupied. But she's not a huge hugger, and I think I've seen her cry twice ever. So when she does, I always just end up sitting there like an idiot.

"I'm really sorry, April. That sucks."

"That's the thing. I'm not allowed to feel like it sucks. It's not like he's just going off to Italy for a year to find himself. He's going to serve the country and do this great noble thing. And I know it's great. And I know it's noble. And that's all Mom and Dad ever talk about, so if I freak out, it's like I'm anti-patriotic. And I'm not."

"I know."

"I'm just scared. That's all. It's not a huge thing."

"Well, it kind of is," I say.

She rolls her eyes. "That doesn't help. Don't make this bigger than it is. My brother is leaving and it's fine. I don't want to talk about it anymore." When I catch her eye, it's like she's saying, *Not to you anyway. You weren't even there when I found out.*

I feel a sharp stab of shame in the pit of my stomach, but cover it up with a smile. "Fro yo after this? It cures all, you know."

She smiles back, but it doesn't reach her eyes. "Sure."

22. How to Morph into an It Girl

I sit in front of my computer, scrolling through my blog. It's getting popular, to say the least. The view number is crazy, and my PayPal account is crazier. In fact, when I run the numbers in my head, I'm . . . I'm there. I don't need another dime, as long as my dad and Stacey are willing to contribute a little to the NY fund. And we talked about that at dinner last night for like an hour. Well. *I* talked about it. Their contribution has been confirmed. A huge smile spreads across my face and I twirl around in my office chair a couple times, then get back to the keyboard.

I shuffle through a couple questions. DELETE. DELETE. Save for later. And then I'm done. For the money, this has been next to no hard labor. I smile, pleased with my entrepreneurial genius. But the joy is short-lived. I hear a knock at my front door, and my stomach drops. I know before going downstairs who it is.

"Hey, Seth," I say when I open it. He's in a heavy coat. Snow is swirling around outside and I can feel the chill sweep into the house, snaking around my arms and legs.

"Can I come in?"

"Sure."

He avoids looking at me when he walks past me into the entryway. "You wanna come upstairs?" I ask.

"Okay." He slips off his jacket and hangs it by the door, then walks up the stairs, trying way too hard to seem nonchalant.

I breathe deeply in and out and follow him up, fidgeting more as we get closer to my room and the inevitable confrontation that lies within.

"How's your nose?" I ask. It's red still, and somewhat purple. And his left eye looks a little weird. It's only been a day, though, so I don't know what I expected.

"Fine. What do you mean 'how's my nose?'"

I heave a giant sigh and sit in my computer chair. "I saw the whole thing. Between you and Drew."

He nods, not looking nearly as surprised as I assumed he would. "I thought I saw a glimpse of blonde fleeing the scene when I got up."

"So," I say.

"So," he parrots.

"What do you want to do?"

He looks out the window for a minute, then back at me. "I mean, I don't want to break up. At least I don't think I do."

I swallow hard, trying like the devil to get past this giant lump in my throat. "I'll tell you anything. Ask. I swear I'm not going to lie to you."

He looks me hard in the eye. "What happened the other night? You slept over?"

I should have figured he'd start there, but honestly, I was hoping he'd do this lie-detector style. Start with some test questions. What color is the sky? What month is it? What's your full name? Do you enjoy kissing me?

"I was just having a sucky day. Really sucky. Just parent stuff, and April and I were on the outs—"

"Who's April?" he asks.

That catches me off guard. How can my boyfriend not even know who April is? Unless . . . holy crap, I haven't mentioned her name or hung out with her at all since we've been together. That hits me like a punch to the gut.

"Uh, April, she's my best friend."

"I thought Drew was your best friend."

"Well, yeah, Drew is my best guy friend. April is my best girl friend. There's a big difference."

"Anyway . . ." he prompts.

"Yeah. Anyway." I look down at my fingers, fidgeting furiously. I wish he was holding them. "April and I were going through some stuff. And my mom is just . . . well, she's not like your mom. So that sucked, too, and it was really late at night but I was about to totally lose it, so I climbed up on my roof and started crying and Drew heard and felt bad. So he let me come over and hang out. And I fell asleep. That's it. I swear, he didn't try anything. And I was fully clothed."

"Was he?"

". . . No. But he wasn't naked either."

Seth sits, then, leaning back against the wall for a little while, kneading his temples. "I am just so not okay with this."

"I know."

"And *what* is going on with you two? He loves you. You say you don't love him. But then you go over and spend the night in his *bed*, which by the way, is something he says has been going on for two years. Is that true?"

"Yes. Yes, but shouldn't that tell you that it meant nothing when I went over there the other night? We have *never* slept together, except, well, literally. But you can ask him and he'll tell you. It's just something I'm used to."

"Do you get how screwed up it is, though? If you found out I was spending the night at Taylor's house, even though we've never had sex, you'd be pissed."

"I know I would. I'd probably dump you, honestly. I guess . . . I guess I'm just banking on you being more tolerant than me."

He scrapes his teeth over his lip, hands lazily clasped over his knee. "I don't know if I can just 'be tolerant' of this, Renley."

I feel tears pricking at the back of my eyes and look away.

"I'm really sorry," I say weakly.

"Please don't cry."

"I'm just so stupid. Like, what is wrong with me? I've been crushing on you since forever, and after two weeks I'm already screwing it up for a guy I don't even want to be with."

He looks up at me, a glimmer of hope in his eyes, and I swallow back the tears I am refusing to let come. "You don't? You can look at me and honestly tell me you don't want to be with him?"

I stare him in the eye. "Seth, I *don't* want to be with Drew. I want you."

"I don't know."

"It was a stupid mistake. Something I did just because it's familiar and I'm not used to having a boyfriend. But I know that's messed up and I'm not going to do it again. I swear. And if you want to break up with me, I get it. It sucks, but I get it."

"I don't want to break up with you, Renley."

"You don't?"

He stands then. "No, I don't. I'm crazy about you. I just don't want to wake up and find out I've been dating a girl who's not over someone else. Not if I'm going to let myself fall for you."

"That's not going to happen."

He rubs the back of his neck and looks out my window at the snow falling gently. "I need to think about some stuff, okay? And I think you do, too."

"I don't—"

"Yeah. You do. If you want to be with Drew, please, be my guest. But I need you to figure it out. Okay?"

I bite my lip and nod.

"See you in class."

"Yeah."

I sit there, picking at my jeans, rehashing everything, thinking. Frick. What am I gonna do?

§

I walk to school the next morning. It's freezing, but the alternative was asking Seth for a ride, and I want to give him at least until cooking before he needs to face me. I don't want to pressure him into making any . . . hasty decisions. So I walk in the cold and cling to his letter jacket.

I eat lunch with April for the first time since Seth and I got together. It's pretty nice, or it would be if it weren't for the sick feeling in my stomach. That horrible, knotting dread.

I suffer through English, knot just tightening harder in my stomach, then head slowly to cooking, like someone going to face the firing squad. Seth's already there when I walk in, standing in his spot beside mine. I slink in beside him and he looks my way.

"Hey," he says.

I look up at him and say quietly, "Hey."

Mr. Cole starts class then. It's a lecture day so we can't even whisper to each other and fake like we're cooking, but Seth reaches over and brushes my fingers with his, and I don't think it's an accident. So that's gotta be a good sign.

I fidget and pay no attention whatsoever for the length of cooking, both dreading and very much looking forward to the end of class.

Seth takes my hand when the bell rings and we head out to the courtyard. We both sit on the concrete, doing that weird eye-avoidance awkward thing until he finally speaks.

"Do you know me, Renley?"

I blink. "What?"

"Do you know me, really? I'm asking you to pick here, between Drew and me, and I want you to make an informed decision."

"I . . . I think I do."

He peers at me and reaches absently for my fingers, fiddling with them. "Did you know I play soccer?"

"No. Tell me. I want to know."

"Okay. I play soccer, and I'm decent at it. I'm Jewish. Obviously. My parents met in the army. Uh, let's see. I'm into hiking. And, dirty little secret, I'm super into Magic, the card game."

I raise my eyebrows. "Seriously?"

"Seriously."

"Your parents met in the army? That's kind of awesome."

He grins.

"Okay, what position do you play in soccer?"

"Center forward."

"Are you on the team?"

He shakes his head. "Shabbos. Got too hard to coordinate never going to practice or games after sundown on Friday. Schools can't have games on Sundays because of religion, but Friday night or Saturday morning? They can indeed."

"What about the Jewish thing? You, like, can't eat pork and have to wait until you're married to have sex?"

He side-eyes me. "Yes. Judaism in a nutshell. No pigs, no fornicating. You got it." Oh, the saltiness in his voice. Just everywhere.

I hit him. "Shut up. That's not what I meant."

He smiles and looks up from my hands. "So. That's me. Now you know."

I lean back against the red wall of the school. "Now I know."

"So. What, then?"

I tighten my grip on his hand. "Seth, I'm not with Drew, I don't want to be with Drew. I want to be with you."

He looks straight into my eyes. "You sure?"

"I'm sure."

He reaches up and takes my face in his hands, then whispers, "Okay," and meets my lips with his. "You want to get out of here?"

"Yes," I say. "Yes I do."

He takes my hand and we cross the parking lot.

"I know this little burger place. Everyone's there right now."

I have no clue who "everyone" is.

"Sounds good to me."

When we pull up, I can see through the window who "everyone" is. It's basically a collection of all the kids everyone talks *about*, but no one actually talks *to*. I recognize several of the kids from the party forever ago.

"Come on," Seth says, and we walk hand in hand into the restaurant. I see Taylor Krissick a couple booths down from where we take our place and if looks could kill . . . yeah, I don't think I need to finish that statement.

"Hey, Seth! And Renley, right?" It's the girl from the party—the pretty Latina one. I wiggle my fingers at her and then my eyes widen. Oh no. She knows my name (which shocks me to my core, for the record), and I . . . have no idea what hers is. I want to crawl under the table.

She laughs at the look on my face. "Sam. No big deal."

"Ugh, I'm sorry. I totally hate it when someone remembers my name and I don't know theirs. I do remember you, though! How on earth do you remember my name, by the way?"

Sam and her girlfriends look back and forth at one another and laugh. "How could we not?" Sam says.

I blink.

"Is she serious?" Sam says, to no one in particular. "You're dating Seth, for one, which is pretty much enough. And not only are you dating him, you somehow managed to steal him from *Taylor,* you slut." (She says this with a smile, so I'm not really sure if it's an insult or a really bizarre compliment. A complisult?) "You'll have to tell me how you did that at some point, by the way. And really, look at you. You're like, crazy hot."

I sit there in stunned silence. Sam just laughs, and the other girls with her laugh, too. It's like I've stepped into *The Twilight Zone.* I feel a little pang at the thought, and Drew flashes through my head. But I shove that away. I'd rather focus on the fact that I've apparently been turning into a goddess and had no idea.

"Well, I'm, um, flattered."

She smiles and then turns to the curvy one. "Ugh, Sophie, stop being so rude and get off your phone. You're totally nocializing."

Sophie turns red, a problem that instantly endears her to me, and waggles the phone in Sam's face. "I haven't read this one yet."

"Since when have you needed advice on how to remove a hickey?"

"Since Gary and I made out last night."

"Ew, Gary?"

I'm totally lost, so I turn my focus back to Seth, who's rubbing his fingers over my knee. He's being way more touchy-feely than usual, which I figure is because of our fight. I don't totally get it—I should probably be the one trying to make up for everything. But I'll take it. The girls grab my attention, though, when I hear the words *Sweet Life*.

"You guys still read that?" I say.

"Well, there's some seriously good info on there. Hickeys are tough to cover up," says Sophie.

"You should know, right?" Sam says to me with a big smile.

I narrow my eyes, but shrug it off. Whatever.

Sophie turns her neck to me and I can see the outline of a little mark under her jaw, but barely. She did a good job covering it, apparently using my advice?

"I would *love* to give you an excuse to use some of that info later," Seth whispers into my ear. I feel myself go red and the girls on the other side of the table exchange wicked grins.

"You've seriously never heard of it?" says the tall girl, Ash.

I shake my head. "Well, just the once. I remember you guys talking about it at the bonfire."

Sam pipes back in. "Oh yeah. You were there, huh! Well, you should get on it. I'm sure Seth would appreciate it." She winks at me, and I'm sure the red deepens considerably. "Or maybe you should get Seth access instead. I swear, the tips and tricks are so worth it."

I laugh and let my hand slide under the table, fingers intertwining with Seth's over my knee. He smiles at me, like we're sharing a little secret.

"For the record, I don't think you need *any* help in that department," I say, and he kisses me under my ear. My skin prickles and my heart rate doubles in the span of two seconds.

"Neither do you," he breathes.

I look over and once again catch the eye of Taylor. She is being such a freaking creeper. Like, isn't there anywhere else she can stare? I roll my eyes and the server gets to our table.

"Can I get a strawberry malt?" I ask. Seth holds up two fingers, signaling that he'd like one as well. The rest of the group already has whatever they ordered, which makes my mouth water.

The server gets back pretty fast, and I take a long, slow drink. I see Sam and the others exchange surprised glances and then drink from their own cups, which I notice are full of brown, fizzy liquid. Probably diet.

I'm suddenly self-conscious about my beverage choice, but I can't really turn back now without looking stupid.

So I take another drink. This one doesn't taste quite as good, somehow.

After about five minutes, the girls stand and exit the booth, then stand there, looking expectantly at me.

"What?" I say.

"We're going to the bathroom," says Ash.

"Okay."

"Well, aren't you coming?"

"Uh, yeah. Sure."

I guess I am. And that's the signal. I'm in.

I push my way out of the booth and follow the girls into the bathroom. All three of them enter the stalls, and just as the doors close, the one behind me opens. I cough.

"Renley, right?" says Taylor, voice sugar sweet and terrifying.

"Yeah. Taylor?"

She leans over the dingy counter, putting on some more lip gloss, and smiles. "Come on, honey. We all know you know my name."

"I—"

She looks over at me, glancing from my head down to my shoes. "What? He hasn't said it while you guys were hooking up yet?"

My mouth falls open. "We haven't hooked up."

"I know," she says. "It's like I've been dating him forever or something. By the way, we're cool, okay? No hard feelings?"

"Okay," I say slowly, grabbing the counter, leaning back away from her.

"Just so you know, though," she says, opening the door, "the other day, when you guys had your little falling out and he needed to 'think,' he came to see me." She smiles viciously and leaves.

My eyes widen and all the girls exit the stalls at the same time.

"Ugh, she is the *worst*," says Sam.

"Yes," says Sophie. "We've been, like, dying for them to break up for ages."

They turn to leave and Ash smiles, pulls her hands out of the sink, and flings them, totally dripping, in my direction. More than once.

I throw my hands in the air and glare at her, water spray all over my chest and face, little droplets in my hair.

They leave without me.

So yeah. I guess I'm in.

DECEMBER

23. How to Cure a Hangover (Among Other Things)

It hurts. Everything hurts. I kind of want to die, except I can't imagine my last moments on earth feeling like *this*. I reach for the Advil I've kept stocked by the bed since last night, just in case, and take two, then gulp down an entire glass of water. What did Google say? A Gatorade? I don't even care; I don't want a Gatorade. I don't want anything. Except to die. And here we are again.

My dad knocks on the door and, I swear, he has never done anything in his life with more gusto. My head throbs harder with every stupid knock.

"Whaaaaaaaat?" I moan.

He cracks the door open. "Honey? Are you feeling okay?"

"No," I say, face stuffed into my pillow. *And freaking talk quieter.*

He tiptoes into my room and sits on the edge of the bed. "What's the matter?"

"Nothing. I just have a headache. And my throat is so dry. I just need some Advil and a nap." I close my eyes. "Can you turn the light down?"

He gets up and flicks the light off, then comes back to the foot of my bed. "Do you have a fever?" He moves to feel my head.

"No. Please don't touch me. Don't."

He stops short and frowns, sniffing the air. "Is that . . . Leelee, is that alcohol?"

"Dad, just go away. Please."

"Is that alcohol on you? Have you been drinking?"

"No." I turn my head back into my pillow. I can feel Dad coming closer, smelling again.

"This is beer. You've been drinking. I know it."

"Who cares?"

"I care. This is dangerous behavior. I thought you were getting better when you stopped sleeping with that boy—"

"Ugh, I never slept with him, Dad—"

"—but now you're off at some party getting drunk? Was Seth there?"

Oh no. Shattering the image of the golden boy. "Yes. He was. But he didn't drink."

Dad furrows his brow and rubs the back of his head. "He . . . he let you do this?"

"Yes. I asked his permission and then I drank allll the alcohol after he gave me his blessing."

Dad shakes his head. Sarcasm does not go over well when you think your daughter is turning into a miscreant. "You can't be doing this."

"Go away."

"Leelee—"

"Go. Away."

"I . . ." he raises his hand, then lets it fall back to the bed, and steps slowly out of the room, shoulders slumped. Normally, I would feel bad. But there's a certain point of misery you hit that is your maximum capacity. Beyond that, nothing. So I don't have the room to feel guilty. I just have room to feel this stupid headache and this stupid throbbing throat and all of this ridiculousness that was brought on by last night. Which is something else I don't want to think about. But I will. Because, obviously, I hate myself.

About a week after Seth and I got things figured out, Sam called him up and invited us to this party at her house. It was supposed to be this amazing thing and "everyone" was going to be there. This time, at least, I knew who "everyone" was. They were all the people we'd been spending the last week with, which still feels kind of unreal to me.

So, Saturday night (last night) rolled around, and we headed over. It was like the classic party scene out of every teen movie ever made. Cars everywhere, kids outside, making out in the dark, ignoring the snow everywhere.

Seth and I made our way inside immediately, 'cause it was freezing. Who would pick to make out outside and freeze when they could be inside? I didn't get it; I still don't.

"Renley!" Sam squealed as we walked inside. She ran across the crowded room, writhing with bodies, and threw her tiny arms around my neck, like we'd been the best of friends for years, not days. And like she didn't secretly hate me and call me various names for sexually promiscuous girls all the time.

"Sam!" I said back, trying to edge equal enthusiasm into my voice.

"So glad you could make it. You look so hot. Like crazy hot."

I did look pretty great. These pants I'd chosen made my butt look supernaturally amazing, and the top clung to all the right places, showing just the right amount of boob and stomach.

"And you look like you got your outfit straight out of *Vogue*," I said.

She smiled brightly and grabbed my hand. "Let me get you a beer, sexy. Or a shot. You want a shot of something?"

I followed her into the kitchen. Where on earth did she find all this alcohol? I swear, she must have bought out an entire agave farm, there were so many shots of tequila sitting out on the kitchen bar.

She got me a clean shot glass and poured me straight tequila. I watched pretty closely, by the way, half-afraid she would put something in my drink if I blinked. But that was unlikely, as I was fairly sure none of these girls actually hated me. They just all treated each other like crap.

"Here," she said, sprinkling a little salt on my arm and handing me a slice of lime. She did the same to her arm. "Lick the salt."

She licked it and I mimicked her.

"Shot!" she yelled.

I tossed my head back and poured the shot down my throat. It burned. Holy wow, it burned.

"Lime!"

She sucked on the lime and grimaced, and I bit into mine with fervor, then shook my head hard, puckering my lips, my eyes . . . I think my cheeks even puckered.

Seth laughed. "Starting out with the hard stuff, I see."

I blinked hard and shook my head again. Wow.

"I've . . . whoa. That goes to your head fast, huh?" I said.

Seth grabbed my elbows, steadying me, and Sam laughed a foggy kind of laugh. "Another. Let's do another."

We repeated the process, and by shot number two, I already felt unsteady. My brain was getting fuzzy, and the rest of me felt warm and weird.

"You drinking?" I asked Seth.

"Nope. DD. You drink what you want though."

"I think I'm good. Whoa, I feel weird." *Maybe I shouldn't be done, though*, I thought. Several of the blog questions I had thrown away started scrolling through my mind. I landed on "How to Cure a Hangover." I wondered how much cash that would bring me.

I'd actually researched it already, just in case. On some level, I think I'd gone there intending to get wasted. I breathed in and shook out my arms and head. "Okay, Sam, what else you got?"

"You want to get drunk?"

"Yes," I said, still feeling kind of wobbly. "Yes I do."

"Wait here," she said, eyes sparkling.

"What are you getting her?" Seth called out.

Sam didn't respond; she just left for a few minutes and came back with something iced. She handed it to me and Seth snatched it away and touched it to his lips. "A Long Island? Come on, Sam. Renley's never had more than a drink of beer in one setting."

Sam shrugged. "She said she wanted to get drunk."

"Well, yeah. Drunk. Not alcohol poisoning."

I grabbed the glass from Seth. "I can take care of myself, *Dad.*" Then I took a long drink. Holy crap. I thought the tequila was strong. Maybe I should have eaten more.

"Maybe slow down a little," Sam said, laughing.

"Where are you getting all this, seriously?" I asked, speech slurring already. I was such a lightweight, it was embarrassing.

"My parents have a fully stocked bar downstairs. We're gonna empty it tonight. They won't even care."

I nodded, the slight head movement making me want to fall over, then I stumbled out of the kitchen and into the crowd of people. They were all grinding against one another, smoothly sliding here and there. The bass thumped in my chest, vibrating everything. I fell into the middle of the crowd, Seth behind me, and took another swig. At this point, I was starting to become less and less aware of what was going on around me.

I turned around and smiled dreamily up at Seth. "Come on. Dance with me."

He grinned down at me, letting his hands fall to my waist and clasp around them. Then I shimmied down his body and back up, fingers playing in his hair.

He tilted his neck back and closed his eyes, so I slid down him and up again, then took another drink. Warmth. Fuzziness everywhere.

I bit my lip when Taylor walked by. I noted a hint of sadness in her eyes when she saw us dancing and that made me feel somewhat guilty beneath the fog of alcohol. Aside from a couple passive-aggressive looks and comments, she'd never been anything but nice to me. But the alcohol took over pretty quickly and she didn't matter. And a couple songs later, it didn't matter when I bumped into her crying in the bathroom either.

After a lot of dancing and avoiding Taylor, one too many times bumping into people, and half a Long Island iced tea downed, I leaned up and whispered sloppily into Seth's ear, "Let's go upstairs. It's too crowded down here."

He looked a little uneasy, shifting his weight back and forth, but there was no way, with me feeling like this, that I wasn't going to make some bad decisions that night. And he was going to make them with me.

He let me lead him up the stairs, like I knew he would, and the second we got behind a door, I basically attacked him. I'm not proud of this—apparently drunk Renley is sexually aggressive, crazy Renley. But at the time, it seemed hot. I still hadn't brought up Taylor's stupid comment about them from the diner, and I didn't intend to.

What I intended to do was win. And somehow, I figured this would accomplish that.

I was all over him, tongue overtaking his mouth, hands grabbing and clawing everywhere, stripping off his shirt. I realized then that I'd never seen him shirtless before. What a crime.

"Hey," he said against my mouth. "You wanna slow down? I just don't know if this—"

And it was at that point that I distinctly remember stripping. Yeah. We'd been dating for like three weeks, so that was great. But it got him to stop talking. And when I was down to jeans and a bra, his mouth just hung open.

"What were you saying?" I slurred, smiling. I think I liked the whole unbelievably drunk feeling at the time, but now it just feels uncomfortable. When you're not 100 percent in control of what you're doing, the next morning is . . . embarrassing, to say the least.

Before Seth could answer me, I was making out with him again—assaulting him, more like. But eventually he pulled back. "Renley, you really need to chill. Not that I don't *love* kissing you. And this is awesome. But, you're just . . . you're really drunk. And I'm really not. I'm not going to take advantage . . . and seriously? You're taking another drink?"

Yes I was. I wasn't going to take any chances that I wouldn't wake up with a hangover. (That was so stupid.)

I sat on the bed, staring up at him with puppy dog eyes, then pouting, twirling my hair with a finger.

He sat beside me and put his arm around me. "Listen, don't be embarrassed. You just have a low tolerance. And low alcohol tolerance plus tequila plus a Long Island is a bad combination."

I kissed him on the cheek. Then the ear. Then that little hollow just below the ear. "So you want me to stop?" Another blog question I'd discarded ran through my head. I'm quite confident that had I not been stupidly intoxicated, the next decision is one I would not have made. But I was, and I did.

When I reached below his belt, he jumped back. "Renley. I *really* don't know if—"

I reached again, and he stopped protesting.

"You're drunk. I shouldn't . . . we shouldn't . . ." And he leaned back and closed his eyes, mumbling something or other.

And that's about all I remember. I know he took me home, and I know I was still awake when he did, because there are two new blog posts on *Sweet Life*. "How to Give a . . . Well, You Know." And "How to Steal Another Girl's Guy." Not that that's anything I did on purpose, but after last night, I must have felt like my expertise on the subject was pretty solid.

For being as hammered as I was, the posts are actually pretty well written, but it will be a couple hours and several homemade remedies before I can blog about this hangover.

I feel pretty crappy right now, in general. We didn't go all the way, just, like, second base and a half. Is that what you'd call it? And that, and knowing I went further than I wanted to, honestly, for what? A blog? Combined with the awful pounding in my head, I think the last twenty-four hours fall decidedly in the "not at all worth it" camp. But whatever. It's done. And I'm gonna get paid for it. End of story.

I pull the covers over my pounding head then and fall asleep.

24. How to Sink a Three-Pointer

When I wake up, I still feel kind of gross. The alcohol sweat and slightly less painful headache don't help, and neither does rehashing last night's mistakes over and over. I wonder if Seth thinks I'm totally disgusting now.

I've missed like three texts and/or calls from April, but she can wait. I'm still totally exhausted.

I take another Advil and quietly walk down the stairs in my socks, searching for Gatorade. Might as well give it a shot and make last night worth it. Ugh, shot. Never. Again.

My dad doesn't even look up from his newspaper, though I pass so close to him, our shoulders almost brush. It must be somewhat hard to deal with, thinking your daughter is some sort of party-hardy, alcoholic super-slut. So I just don't say anything and leave him to process the information.

The Gatorade feels good on my throat, though it doesn't do a whole lot to get rid of the tequila/rum/gin/triple-sec/vodka smell that won't get out of my nostrils or my pores. So I gingerly step into the shower, letting the hot water steam everything away. I wash my hair like three times and do the same thing to my body, dying to get rid of the smell and the ick.

The water is as hot as I can stand and feels amazing running down my back. For a second, the headache even goes away. When I'm done and clean, I wrap up in a towel and head to my room. The feeling of complete and utter suck is dissolving, which is nice. Maybe by tomorrow, I'll be a fully functioning human again.

ᕼ

Tomorrow comes, and I am. Honestly, by last night I was feeling pretty good. Having never had a hangover (or anything close) before, I have no idea if it's because of my various concoctions or just because they go away after that amount of time, generally.

It doesn't matter. I'm going to post about it. There's no way I'm dealing with the crap I dealt with all day yesterday and getting nothing for it. So I make up a quick list of remedies I used (sleep, Gatorade, Advil, a shower—nothing revolutionary, really, aside from this Sprite-and-Menudo combination that Sam swears by and I'm too chicken to try) and post. Admittedly, this one is kind of lazy. Possibly not worth the nominal amount I'm charging for looking at it. Whatever. What's done is done.

I go into the bathroom and splash cold water on my face, then toss my unbrushed hair into a ponytail. I pull on a pair of sweats, a thin long-sleeve, and tennis shoes and head toward the door. There's snow on the ground and I feel ice forming in my veins just looking out the window, but school's off for a pre-break teacher wrap-up and I need to run today or do something that's not in the house. So I push open the door and head out into the fray.

I feel an immediate mixture of regret and happiness when the little snowflakes float and spin around me, landing in my hair, on my nose, coating me in white that turns instantly to water. I won't run for long; I haven't been serious about it since middle school so I only ever really run with Drew anymore. It's been too many weeks since I did that, and the cold air burns my throat and lungs. The long, quick strides I'm making do the same to my muscles. It feels good, though, somehow, in a kind of masochistic way. I make a loop around the neighborhood, snow crunching beneath my feet, lightly coating the tracks I leave behind.

I'm out there for maybe five minutes, but it feels like longer. I wish I could run longer, but the cold kind of sucks. So I round one more corner, knowing it will take me back home.

When I near my house, I can hear the sound of a basketball bouncing on the pavement, hollow and loud. I frown and turn my face to the right, then realize I'm passing Drew's house. He sees me and picks up the ball, then waves.

I furrow my brow and slow, then come to a stop. "Hey," I say, testing the waters.

"Hey," he says, and he tosses me the ball.

I can't stop the smile that comes across my face, the smile that almost hurts because my lips are most likely turning blue. I dribble a couple times on the sidewalk, then hold the ball close to my chest, squatting down, taking in the distance up, out, the slight incline of the driveway. And shoot. Nothing but net.

Drew catches the rebound and dribbles back to the grass, looking at me, a challenge in his eyes. I stare longingly at my window, then back at Drew. My desire to be with my best friend again outweighs my wants for comfort so I jog up to meet him and post up—crouch, hands out. I don't know how long it's been since we played basketball together. We used to play all the time when we were kids, though, and it takes just a few seconds to become acclimated again.

He looks at my eyes, leaning slightly to the right, then to the left, switching hands. His breath comes in visible puffs, clouding the air in front of me. My eyes are darting every which way—I can't decide where he's going. Then he twitches to my right, so I go to the left, and he nearly barrels into me, ball bouncing down the almost half-court to the basket. Despite my best efforts, I'm just a lot shorter than him, so a layup is nothing, easy.

"Still got it, I see," I say.

"Oh yeah. I'm going pro, I think."

I take the ball and back up to the edge of the concrete. "I gotta be honest," I say. "I thought you'd hold out a little longer."

"What do you mean?"

I shove past him, heading toward the basket, and when I shoot, he leaps up, knocking it out of the air and catching it, then racing back to half-court.

"I mean, I thought you'd make me leave you alone for more than a week before I was allowed to come back over."

He jumps up gracefully, just a couple inches from the ground, sinking the shot, and it's mine again.

"Yeah, well, basketball is boring by yourself."

"True."

I don't even dribble this time. I back up several steps into the snow-covered grass and shoot from there, smirking when it sinks.

"Show-off," he says, grinning.

"I've missed you," I say quietly as he walks over to the gravel behind the hoop. He stops for a split second at that.

"What, Seth not entertaining enough for you?"

"Oh, he's entertaining enough. Things are good there."

"So I've heard," he says, reaching down to pick up the ball. He heads up to half-court and dribbles, feinting past me down to the hoop and shooting. It glances off the rim, and against all odds, I'm the one who catches it. I pop it back up and off the rim it goes again, straight to me. One more shot and it circles the drain, then falls through the net.

"Bad move, Eisler."

I raise an eyebrow.

"You didn't take it back before you shot. My point."

I glower at him. Stupid. But correct. "Fine. I don't need technicalities to beat you anyway."

"Oh, I doubt that," he says, firing a shot from farther back than I made it earlier—and sinking it.

He passes it to me, and I run past him, almost halfway to the center of the yard. I try to ignore the shivering in my arms from the cold, and he just stands there, noticing, I'm sure, and crossing his arms skeptically.

"There's no way you're making it from there."

"Have faith, sir."

"It's a three-point shot. And the cold is getting to you."

I twist the ball in my hands, feeling the weight of it, visualizing it going through the net.

"Let's bet. You make it, you win. You fail, I win."

"What's the wager?" I say, teeth chattering now. Not enough movement, and snow, and the sweat I've accumulated is getting cold.

"Well, I doubt we're playing strip rules." He winks and a happy warmth floods through me. This is normal. This is us, from before everything.

I shake my head. "Not in this weather."

He eyes the thin fabric covering my arms and rolls his eyes. "Fine. I win, you're coming in and we're watching *Twilight Zone*."

"And if I win?"

"I'll order Chinese, too, and pay for it."

"You're on," I say.

I stare up at the backboard again, dribbling a couple times on the wet grass. Stupid idea; now the ball's all slick and impossible to hold onto. But I power through, gripping it firmly and crouching, then bouncing up. Left hand steady, right hand tosses and spins it. I watch as it glides through the air, with the most perfect topspin I've ever seen on a ball.

It thwacks the backboard dead center, then bounces back out to the front rim and through the net. I laugh loudly, intentionally obnoxious.

"You!" I shout. "You owe me food, Calloway."

"I humbly accept my defeat," he says, gathering up the ball and putting his arm around my shoulders. I probably shouldn't be eating Chinese; it's super fattening. But I'm hungry, and this feels nice. Too nice? I don't know.

When we get closer to his door, he says casually, "Hey, I've been meaning to talk to you."

And the pulse in my wrist starts going erratic. He still reads the blog, I know he does. And I don't want to talk about it. Not with him. I don't know what I'm so terrified of, but I can't. I'm totally paralyzed by those innocuous little words. I freeze.

"What?" he asks.

"Nothing, it's just, I just completely forgot, I have something."

He narrows his eyes and takes his arm off my shoulders. "What?"

"With Stacey."

"Oh yeah, I'll bet."

"No, I do. I . . . I have to go. We'll talk later, okay?" *No we won't.*

He purses his lips and goes inside without another word. Stacey. What a ridiculous lie. Seth would have fallen for it. Sam would have fallen for it. But this is Drew.

I don't care. This is something we can't discuss, something I don't want to discuss, and something I shouldn't have to. And I'm choosing to feel good about today. Because everything felt normal for just a little while. I'm getting Drew back, and despite the awkwardness, that makes everything okay.

25. How to Get a Date to Prom

A message from Seth. **Hey hey.**

Come pick me up. I miss you

Done.

I'm unbelievably relieved that he hasn't brought up the incident at the party. Not crazy, drunk Renley, not the below-the-belt action that I basically forced on him, nothing. And because of that, I'm not dreading seeing him. I'm just excited.

I run a straightener through my hair and do my makeup—something I can now do masterfully within about five minutes. Hot jeans, nice top, his letter jacket (which still makes me kind of giggle), and I'm good to go by about the time he gets here.

"Hey, beautiful," he says, and he kisses me on the cheek, lingering. I blush.

We head out and over to his house. When we get there, I follow him upstairs and into his room, realizing I've never actually been in here before. That's weird.

"So, this is your room," I say, running my fingers over the dresser.

"This is it." He stretches out his arms, mock-presenting it to me.

It smells fresh in here, maybe even better than mine. And apart from one crumpled T-shirt in the corner and a slightly disorganized computer desk, it's clean. Really clean.

"I'm impressed," I tell him truthfully.

"My mother has trained me well."

She really has. He sits down on his bed and I start to sit beside him, but he pulls me onto his lap. I laugh and he kisses me.

"So, about the other night . . ."

Oh no. I should have known he'd bring this up. "Yeah."

"You feeling okay?"

"Oh, I'm good now. I mean, the day after . . ."

"I kind of figured. I should have brought you Sprite and menudo, probably . . . I know, but Sam swears by it."

I chuckle. "Trust me. That would not have helped."

He fidgets a little, and I can feel his fingers moving nervously against each other on my back. "I wanted to talk about . . . the other stuff that went down."

Awesome. Either he's going to think I'm a total skank and be turned off forever or he's gonna figure I just do that all the time and expect it to happen again. Either way is not good.

He looks up at me, and all I want to do is crawl in a hole and stay there until summer comes.

"I mean, here's the thing. It was good. Really good. Amazing actually."

Okay, option #2 it is.

He continues, "But it's just . . . it's not something I'm totally comfortable with. And I feel like a total asshole since you were drunk. I don't know."

I breathe a giant sigh of relief.

"I mean, I'm not completely blameless here," I say. "You protested. I was drunk. But not so drunk I don't remember that. Shit."

Seth shrugs, hand on the back of his neck, and looks at the floor. "Either way. I'm just not . . . I don't want you to think I'm not into you, or I'm a prude or anything. I'm just not exactly ready to take this there yet. Know that my entire body is protesting this decision big time, by the way. Like, I'll probably hate myself when you go home. Just . . . okay, now you're not saying anything. Do you hate me?"

I laugh. "Hate you? I was thinking the same thing. I'm super embarrassed about everything, and I'm just not that experienced and ugh, I'm so glad you feel the same way. Kind of surprised. But glad. I don't hate you. I—" I stop short, not totally sure how to finish that sentence. Love you? Like you? Kind of have a crush on you?

He waits there for a while, then says quietly, "I love you, too."

I didn't actually tell him I loved him, so the answer is a little presumptuous. Nonetheless, butterflies are everywhere in my stomach, fluttering all over the place, crashing into each other.

"You do?" I say, eyes giant and round.

"Yeah. I know we haven't been together that long, but I do."

I reach my palm out to his cheek and he kisses me deeply, giving me that feeling in the pit of my stomach. One so delicious I never want him to stop. Then he flips me over onto his bed and kisses me again, lips moving down my throat and back up to my ear.

"Come to prom with me," he whispers in my ear.

"What?"

He raises up, running his fingers up and down my waist. "Come to prom with me."

"It's all the way in April."

"So?" he asks, grinning and dipping down to kiss me again. His kisses are freaking intoxicating. "You planning on breaking up with me before then?"

"You wish you were getting off the hook that easy." It's like his lips are a magnet for my mouth. I can't help kissing him when they're there. Right. There.

"So come. It's my senior prom. I'll pick you up in a limo"—he kisses my neck—"you can wear a fancy dress"—kisses my ear—"I'll dance with you all night." Down to my throat again.

"I can't even think with you doing that."

"Good." He keeps doing what he's doing and my brain stays delightfully fuzzy.

"Okay, I'll go." I smile. His lips are totally hypnotizing. Something in the back of my mind niggles at me, but I ignore it and go back to focusing on the sweetest, hottest boyfriend anyone has ever had.

Until I get home. I scroll to my calendar in my phone and stop short when I reach April 29, the day of the senior prom. It's the last day of the New York trip. No, no, no. This can't be happening. What was Mr. Sanchez thinking, scheduling the trip the same freaking week as the senior prom? (Granted, no one in the math club is a senior this year. Still, though.)

I can't go. I throw the phone on my bed, like taking vengeance on the electronic device will bring me some satisfaction. I can't believe I have to miss what could potentially be the most romantic, amazing night of my life to go see the math museum and planetarium. What a loser.

I lie back on the bed, dreaming about Seth's arms around my waist, slow dancing with him, kissing him. I'd wear a long dress, maybe sparkly. Spaghetti straps. Probably an updo. Maybe down and curly. Halfway in between?

And then I think about New York. A bunch of kids from the math club who often forget to wear deodorant, exploring mathematical wonders and talking about differential equations and string theory. Whoop-de-do.

When it comes down to it, I know what I really want to do. But it would kill April. It would be horrible. I can't cancel on her. I can't.

I lie there for a while, considering. Would she care, really? She'd be there with Cash. It would probably be easier for them to be all over each other if I wasn't there, honestly. She might be relieved. And it's not like I'd be canceling just to go on a date to like, a concert or something. This is prom. His senior prom. If I don't go with him, he'll find another date. Someone else who would be more than willing to dress up and dance with him and stick her tongue down his throat. A picture of Sam with him at prom comes into my mind. Then, even worse, Taylor. I feel sick.

April would understand, wouldn't she?

I spend the next three hours agonizing over what to do. And then I pick up the phone.

Hey.

Hey stranger. How you been?

Good. Thinking.

That could be dangerous ;) April says.

It's about NY.

She takes a little while to respond. Then writes,

okkkkkkk

I don't know if I'm coming.

Silence. For, like, twenty minutes. I don't know what to do. Text her again? Call? Maybe her phone died. Then there's a knock on the door. A knock that could wake the dead. I hear it slam open and April shrieks, "Renley!"

I walk hesitantly down the steps to meet her. "Yeah?" I say, voice mousy and weak.

"What do you mean you *don't know* if you're coming?" She's so mad she's shaking. Her hands are curled into fists at her sides. Even her hair looks mad somehow.

"I mean I don't know."

"Haven't you paid already? At least the first half? It's nonrefundable."

"The deadline's tomorrow," I say, fidgeting.

Her face falls then. "What are you even saying? This is all we've been talking about this entire year. What is this about?"

I suddenly feel very small and very stupid. "It's just . . . Seth asked me to go to prom with him, and—"

"PROM? This is about a *dance*? I can't even . . . I don't even believe this. You're abandoning me to go to a dance for three hours with a guy. This is New York Freaking City, Renley." She grabs my shoulders. "NEW YORK. Do you understand that?"

"I . . . yes. But it's his prom, April. It's not just any dance."

She lets go of me and steps backward, a look of complete disgust on her face. "Who ARE you?"

"Don't be dramatic."

"No," she says. "I want to know what has happened to you. You change your hair, start spending every second of your free time with The Amazing Seth, Greek god, dressing like *that*, and wearing so much makeup you look like a three-dollar hooker—"

"Excuse me. But I don't think you have any room to be calling anyone a hooker, you slut."

She recoils as though I've slapped her. And the guilt feels worse than the zinger feels good. But it's true.

"Slut? *Slut*? I may kiss a lot of guys, Renley. I know I do. But it's freaking fun. And that's it. That's all I've ever done with anyone until Cash, hickey queen. Yeah. Cash. No I didn't tell you. Of course I didn't. And I don't care if you were sleeping with half the school, I would never call you a slut. And I would never treat you the way you've treated me for the last two months. And now *this*? Abandoning New York? Abandoning *me* for some guy? Yeah," she says, hands held out, backing away, "I think I finally see how you and your mom are related."

My eyes fly open wide, and there's a literal pain in my chest like she's stabbed me. "April—" I say, but she flips me off and walks out the front door, slamming it behind her.

26. How to Throw Out Something That Matters

"Hey, are you doing okay?" Seth asks as we hang out in my room. He's running his fingers up and down my back, and I'm just lying there, frustrated.

"I'm fine. It's just . . . nothing. April."

"For being BFFs or whatever you call it, it seems like you guys are on the rocks a lot."

"Yeah. Seems that way." I shake my head, trying not to cry, watching the snow fall slowly outside my window. She's being ridiculous, right? She totally is.

"What are you guys fighting about?"

"Nothing. I don't really want to talk about it." Every time I think about telling Seth what's going on, I feel embarrassed. Like I don't want him to know I gave up going to New York to go to prom with him. I made the right choice. I know that. It's something I shouldn't be embarrassed about. But I am, so I just let him scratch my back and take my side without questioning me.

After about a half hour of back scratching and quiet angst, he slowly gets up from the bed. "I gotta go," he says.

"Don't go."

"I have to." He kisses my forehead. "First night of Chanukah. Plus, I've got this giant trig exam tomorrow. And I know you're a math wizard and all, but studying with you does nothing to help my grades."

I grin wickedly and he smiles back.

"You're still going to school? On Chanukah?"

"Minor holiday. So yeah, alas, school must go on."

"Bummer."

"I'll see you, love," he says, heading through my door.

"See you."

And he leaves me alone to wait out the evening in solitude. I spend most of it just listening to music and contemplating, which makes for a fairly boring (and depressing) night, but around ten o'clock, I see something outside my window that catches my attention. At first, I frown. That can't be right. But no. That aqua blue in her hair is unmistakable. April is sitting on Drew's doorstep in the snow.

He has his arm around her and they're talking like they're old friends. Since when did that happen? Drew never has girls who aren't me over unless . . . holy shit. No.

I feel sick to my stomach all of a sudden and double over. I might actually throw up right here on my carpet. Are they . . . did she sleep with him? For what? Revenge? Tears spring to my eyes and blur my vision so badly I can barely see out the window. But I have to. So I wipe them furiously and stare out of the glass again.

He has his arm around her and he's giving her a hug, a close hug. I hurt. Everywhere. Part of me doesn't even want to watch, but it's like a car accident. You drive past knowing there's wreckage and broken glass and maybe blood. And of course you hope no one died. But if someone did, part of you wants to see it. So you slow down and you stare. I stare.

Then he does something worse than the hug: she wraps her arms around herself, and he leans over and says something to her, then shrugs his shoulders and slips off his jacket and hands it to her. It's like someone has taken a serrated knife and twisted it in my gut.

He gave her his freaking jacket.

That sick feeling hits again and I back away from the window, reeling. This cannot be happening. They cannot be doing anything together. April would never do that to me. Drew would never do that. Would he?

I'm drawn back to the window again, and they're standing now, hugging each other tightly. He walks her to her car and she takes off the coat and hands it to him. Then she drives off. Good. She'd better, or this would be a double murder.

The second she drives off, I'm sprinting down the stairs. My face is red and hot before the descent even begins. By the time I get to Drew's, I can actually feel smoke rising from my pores.

I bang on his door so hard, I'm surprised nothing splinters. He opens it and his eyes fly open when I shove past him into the foyer.

"You gave her your jacket?" I spit. Those were not the words I'd planned to say.

"What?"

"April. You gave her your jacket?"

"I . . . yeah. It's freezing outside."

I sink down to the tile and wrap my arms around my knees and let forth a cry, sobbing without sound.

"R, I told you I needed to talk to you."

"I had no idea it was about this. About you and . . . ugh, I can't even say it."

He reaches down, lifting me up by the elbow, and leads me into his room.

"Listen. April came by a couple hours ago, saying she needed to talk, and—"

"You don't even like April."

"I never said I didn't like her. I said I didn't know her. Big difference. Anyway, it doesn't matter. She came by and told me about New York."

My face shoots up and I glare at him. "So you what? Pity screwed her?"

His features twist into a mask of confusion. "What? Pity screwed? I didn't touch her," he says, voice rising a decibel. "No, I let her talk to me. She thinks I can make you listen. And she said you abandoned New York to go to a dance? With Seth?"

"Yes. So?" I can hear the venom in my own words. He hasn't accused me yet, not really, but I already want to bolt. Or punch him. I can't decide.

"I thought she was your best friend."

"Well, I thought so too, until she up and decided that if I didn't go on a six-hundred-mile trip with her, we were through."

He's quiet for a while, and his voice is low when he does finally speak. "Do you even hear yourself right now?"

I stare at him, squeezing my knees tighter.

"I'm serious. You're being, well, you're being totally crazy."

I laugh.

"Renley, she's right. You swore you were going, and the day before it was all for sure, you bailed. For a guy. And you know that was bullshit. Does Seth even know?"

"That we're going to prom together? I'd hope so," I say coolly.

"Don't play dumb with me. Does he know you gave up New York for it?"

I don't say a word.

"I'll bet you every cent you've earned from your stupid blog that he doesn't. 'Cause you know he'd tell you you were crazy. Of course April's pissed. I'm pissed. Neither of us has any idea where on earth our best friend has gone."

I roll my eyes. "Oh please, Mr. Melodrama."

He shakes his head. "I still read your blog, you know. And what you've been pulling . . ." He runs his hand through his hair and sits heavily on his bed.

I stand then. "What? Tell me what I've done that's any worse than anything you've ever done."

"This is not about me. This is about you. How to Get Rid of a Hickey? How to Cure a Hangover? How to Give a Hand Job? That's not *you*. And I'll bet you double or nothing that by the end, you didn't even need the money."

I clench my jaw, arms crossed hard over my chest.

"You didn't, did you? Listen, I couldn't care less what you do with Seth behind closed doors. I honestly don't care. And drink whatever you want. Go to whatever parties you want with whomever you want. But do it because *you* want to do it. Not to, what? Please some loyal reader you've never met on the Internet? Or maybe it's the popularity. Is that it? I just don't get it."

I'm fuming. I can feel my blood pressure rising. "What I do is none of your business, Drew."

"You're right. And it's none of cyberspace's business either."

"Look at you, High and Mighty Drew. It's so easy for you to judge me, isn't it? You and April, new best friends, looking down on poor, misguided little Renley. Well I don't need either of you. I'm doing fine on my own."

"Yeah. Seems that way. When was the last time you took the initiative to text April first? You totally forgot about her because you've been so busy being SweetLifeCoach and hanging out with Seth and Sam and the rest of that crowd and you've totally left her behind. And that matters to me. Because you love April. And you're about to lose her completely. Do you get that?"

"I didn't ask for your input on this."

"I beg to differ. I didn't march into your house in the middle of the night, demanding to know why you let someone borrow your jacket."

I don't know why that makes me want to cry again. "Why did you give her your jacket?" I say quietly, rage discarded for just a moment.

Drew sighs and looks right at me, eyes boring into me. "Because she can take care of herself. I don't know her that well, but I know enough to know that. She doesn't walk around, needing everyone else to. But you . . . I'm crazy about you; you know that. But you go through your whole life waiting for someone else to take care of everything for you. You have a problem, you don't just try to figure it out. You get it from someone else. You need money; you turn to your parents and random strangers on the Internet. You never remember a jacket because you just expect me to give you one. You think you need it. And you don't. You're strong. There's nothing wrong with needing someone to take care of you every once in a while, but you don't need it all the time. And until you figure that out, you don't get my freaking jacket."

I just stand there for several seconds, blinking, and turn away.

"I don't want you to lose yourself because of all this," he says.

My nostrils flare and I whip around to face him. "Lose myself. Yeah. I'm drowning in all my *issues*. Because I went further with a guy than I meant to. Because I got drunk at a party and got a group of friends that doesn't include you and April. And because I sometimes forget to wear a jacket. You want to talk about problems? Let's talk about you laying everything that moves. You don't think that's an issue?"

He looks up at me like I'm stupid. "*Of course* it's an issue. How many other guys do you know who sleep with half as many girls as I do? I have problems. But we are not discussing me. We're discussing you. You're destroying everything you care about for a blog. And for that awesome self-esteem boost you get when everyone notices you. Is it worth it?"

He's so self-righteous, I want to throttle him. I stomp out of his room, and he follows me.

"I don't want to threaten you, R," he says softly.

I can feel the blood drain from my face. "What?"

"I don't. Want. To. Threaten you."

"What? You're gonna hit me now?"

He rolls his eyes. "Don't be stupid. I'd never touch you."

"Then what?"

He's quiet, avoiding looking at me. Then his eyes meet mine, and my blood runs cold. I know what he's going to say before he says it. "I'll tell everyone."

"Excuse me?"

"You're turning into someone you hate, doing things you regret as you're doing them. And you're going to lose everyone. I can't let you do that. I'll tell everyone who's really behind that blog, I swear."

"No you won't," I say, voice low and shaking. "You'd never do that to me. You love me."

"Exactly."

I can't even feel an emotion by this point; I'm just numb. Numb and ice. "I see what's really going on here. This isn't about me changing. This is about me choosing Seth over you."

A muscle in his jaw jerks.

"That's it. I'm not the one who's changed. You would *never* have done this to me before. Never." My voice starts to rise. "You just have such a hard-on for me that you can't see past it to realize that *you're* the one who's changed."

He's shaking now, jaw clenched tighter than I've ever seen, eyes hard. "You're right, Renley. I don't care about you at all. I can't see past this *massive erection* I have enough to see that this would hurt you. I've never really loved you, never done a thing for you. Never let you stay all night with me, dying because I couldn't touch you. Never gotten up in the middle of the night to stop you from crying. Never stopped a girl from coming over so you could feel special. You're right. *Totally.*"

I shrug.

His face darkens and his voice is dangerous and low. "Get out."

He doesn't have to tell me twice.

27. How to Remove a Knife from Your Back

I roll over sleepily when the sun streams through my window. I have a slight headache. Not horrible, just from . . . well, the craziness last night, I think. I'm a little annoyed that the first thing that pops into my brain this morning is all of that crap. April and her lovely middle finger. And Drew and his murdery rage-voice.

The only person I want to talk to right now is Seth. He can distract me. So I reach for my cell phone.

Ugh, you would not BELIEVE how cray April is being.

The phone buzzes about thirty seconds after I hit SEND.

I don't care.

I frown and stare at the phone.

?

Stop texting me.

My stomach jumps up and tries to squeeze itself into my throat. I dial Seth's number, or try anyway. I have to enter it four times before I get it right. It rings. And rings. And then his voicemail. I'm shaking everywhere. And I have to be at school in a few minutes.

I get dressed in a panic, rushing a brush over my teeth and another through my hair (though I'm so frazzled, I initially mix them up). I'm trying to convince myself that the adrenaline coursing through me is not because . . . no. I'm not letting myself consider it; I won't think about it. Because he didn't. Drew *didn't*.

I don't want to take the bus. With every fiber of my being, I don't. So I focus instead on that and allow myself to dread the ride, because Dad's car is off-limits when it's at his office and, you know, not here.

So I sprint out to the bus, looking like a crazy person, and get on.

Then one more text from Seth. A forward. It's nothing but a link.

I get to my cell's browser and type the address into the search box, denying over and over what I know is coming. When I navigate there, my hand flies to my mouth.

At the top of the site in big, bold letters, it says: **SWEETLIFECOACH'S IDENTITY REVEALED.**

I'm going to completely lose the nothing I ate this morning. He did it; he actually did it. I shake my head several times in rapid succession, hoping I'm somehow seeing it wrong. But every time I look back at the screen, it's still there.

I scroll down, reading the article feverishly, and finally at the end, my name comes up. "The author in question is none other than one Renley Eisler. Some of you know her, some of you don't. Well, now, I suppose you ALL do."

My stomach is churning, every piece of my body burning hot. I have to fix this.

I practically tumble off the bus and text Seth, knowing he won't pick up if I call.

> **Please, Seth. I have to talk to you. You have to listen to me. I can explain.**

There's radio silence for an agonizing ten minutes, then he writes:

> **Fine. I'll meet you at the school's entrance in a min.**

I'm scraping my hands through my hair, fuzzing it up more than it already is when he shows up, and I remember I haven't touched my makeup, which is embarrassing. And it can't work in my favor. Sex appeal would probably be helpful here.

He doesn't say hello when he enters the hall; he just stalks in and glowers.

I try to give him a hug, and he turns his body so that it's impossible. My arms fall to my sides, matching the crestfallen look on my face.

"Talk," he says.

I swallow hard. I hadn't even considered, in the utter panic of this morning, what to say when he got here. Do

I tell the truth? Lie? I stand there in front of him, mouth agape, until he purses his lips and leans back against the wall, arms crossed. I can feel him shutting down. That's it. Lie it is.

"Seth, that link, it's not true. It's from someone who apparently hates me and wants to destroy my reputation. But I'm telling you, I would never have written some of the things on that site." I try desperately to ignore several dirty looks I get from strangers when they pass. They vacillate between staring at their phones and at my face. They don't matter. They don't matter.

He laughs a callous laugh. "Oh please. Don't lie to me. I'm not stupid. You're trying to tell me it's a coincidence that the day after we do anything at all together, it magically ends up on that blog? The day after I gave you a hickey, 'How to Get Rid of a Hickey.' The day after the party, something about a hand job." He shakes his head, unable to even look straight at me. "And a day or two after that, 'How to Cure a Hangover.'"

"That's totally not—"

"Let me just stop you right there," he says, pushing his hand out at me. "I know it's you. Don't lie to me. The second I hear something else blatantly false, I'm gone. And I'm not coming back. You got that?"

I nod slowly, trying not to hyperventilate, and sit, right in the middle of the hall. I'm starting to feel lightheaded.

"Okay. It's me."

He blows out a resigned breath.

"But I swear, I didn't do it to hurt anyone. And I never meant to hurt you, of all people."

"How about Taylor?" he asks.

"What?"

"Taylor. Did you mean to hurt her?"

"I don't understand . . ."

He pulls out his phone and taps something, then hands it to me. On the screen are the words *How to Steal Another Girl's Guy*. I can feel myself pale.

"You didn't steal me, Renley. Let's just clear that up. I broke up with Taylor because I wanted to, not because of you. You just happened to be my rebound."

I recoil from the sting.

"I know," I say, throat dry. "I know I didn't. I just . . ." I rest my forehead in my palm. "This has all gotten so out of control."

"Why would you do this in the first place?"

"Because I needed money to go to New York with April and the math club, and my dad can't afford to pay for it all." My voice is muffled by my hands.

"The math club? You were going to that? I thought you were going to prom with me."

"Yeah. I just . . . I changed my mind about New York when you asked."

The look on his face when I say that confirms that I shouldn't have told him.

"You're serious? You were going to abandon *New York* to go to a dance with me? No wonder I've been getting so much hate mail from April in the last forty-eight hours."

He trails off and we're both quiet. Then he says, "I just . . . I can't believe this. You 'stole' me, kissed me, did everything with me for money? For a blog? Was any of this ever real for you?"

The look on his face is heartbreaking. Like I've just stomped all over him, and honestly, I probably have. I can't help it; I start to cry. "Yes," I say through the tears. "It was all real, I swear. Just because I wrote about it doesn't mean I didn't have feelings for you. I do; I still do."

He rubs his eye and stands up straight from the wall. "You know what, Renley? I have put up with more from you than I even put up with from Taylor. And for the record, that's saying something. You manipulated me, came this close to cheating on me with another guy, got me punched in the face, lied to me, and broadcast it to the entire world. You know all my friends now know exactly what it's like to get me off with a hand job? Not just anyone. Me."

"Seth, please. If you would just listen—"

"I'm done listening. I honestly don't know why I'm still standing here."

His letter jacket is sitting crumpled on the floor beside me, and he grabs it when he leaves. For a minute after he goes, I can't breathe.

Drew. How could he do this to me? Everyone is going to know. Everyone already does know, probably, and the only ones who don't are the people who are choosing to sleep through the last week of school before break.

I stand up shakily from the ground and hug my back-pack to my chest. And I'm not exaggerating here—*everyone* is staring at me. Everyone besides the kids who don't wear makeup or make out with anyone or go to drunken parties anyway. I slink down to calculus, feeling their stares boring into the back of my head, hearing the little whispers behind my back. Sam and the others won't stop giving me these looks that combine evil and laughter, and I swear, even a couple teachers give me death glares. It's unsettling. I want to throw up.

I'll have to shut down the blog. Maybe even switch schools. I don't know if I can face everyone after all this. I definitely can't go to cooking. So I suffer through the first half of the day and walk home before lunch. For once, I'm happy about the placement of my free period.

It's cold without Seth's jacket.

I'm lying in my bed, slowly dying, thoughts whirring so hard and fast I can't grab hold of a single one. Then there's a knock on my door. A loud one. I stand up just as my dad forces his way in. Maybe he thinks I'm sick since I'm home early and he wants to come comfort me. Maybe he's bringing me some hot chocolate. I could use some of that right now.

The look on his face tells me otherwise.

"What. Is. THIS?" he bellows, throwing a giant stack of papers down to the ground.

I jump up from the bed and take a step back. "I don't know."

He picks a stray one up from the pile and clears his throat. "Step one. Unbuckle the guy's belt. This is a fairly important step, for obvious reasons. Step two—"

I grab the paper from him and hug it close to my chest. "How many did you read?"

"All of them."

I'm going to die. I'm actually going to die. "How did you . . . ?" I know the answer. But something in me needs to hear him say it.

"Drew came over this morning with a stack of papers, right after you left for school."

I gag. "Drew told you? He . . ." I can't even finish a sentence.

"I think I might have misjudged that boy," he says, more to himself than me. "And yes. He did. This behavior. This vulgar writing is not you."

Tears are burning my eyes. "Yes it is, Dad. This is me. This is who I am. And I'm really sorry if you hate me, like everyone else does now."

He picks up another page, one about the hangover, I think, and scans it, grimacing. "Really? Sloppy drunk? Doing shots all night with kids you don't even know? This is you? This is the Renley who's been living with me since she was a baby? The Renley who was so excited to go to the planetarium she didn't stop talking about it until two weeks ago? The Renley who spends her weekends studying calc and hanging out with the Math Club. That's this Renley?"

I choke on the tears welling up in my throat. "Yes."

How to Make Out

He stares at me with Dad-eyes. The ones that say, *I love you, and I'm so disappointed in you I can't take it for another second.* The very worst kind of way to be looked at. People think moms are experts at guilt, but for me, my dad has always been king in that department. He follows the wound up with salt: "I don't know what I'm doing wrong here."

That is the worst. "Dad—"

"No. You're not allowed to give me excuses. Or to explain. Whatever I'm doing here is clearly not working. So you're—you're grounded."

The word sounds so foreign coming from my dad's lips that, at first, I actually don't understand. "I'm what?"

"You're grounded."

"Oh, please." I stand and head to my door, but he reaches out to it and slams it closed. I snap my head over to look at him, eyes like saucers.

"No," he says firmly. "You're grounded. For real. No friends. No phone. Definitely no blogging. This weekend, you can read and do math problems and, you know, think about what you've done."

His lack of experience in this area is somewhat glaring, evident from the uncomfortable look on his face and the fact that, when he leaves me standing there, mouth agape, he doesn't actually take my phone or computer.

I sink slowly onto my bed, contemplating. Grounded. For once in the last five years, I'm being punished. I should be mad. I should be freaking out and cursing the day my dad was born, right? But I don't. I'm not happy, but I'm just . . . not angry with him. It doesn't make sense.

I rub my fingers over my bedspread, trying to process everything that's happened this morning. And when I do, I feel something that doesn't match the texture of my blanket. It's a sheet of paper. Someone with lovely handwriting has written on it. Stacey. Dad must have left it.

Because I have no real desire to defy my dad's declaration, despite its suckiness, I have nothing else to do. So I pick it up.

LeeLee, —I roll my eyes—

I'm under no illusions that you like me. Truthfully, I know you hate me. You've made that clear. And I get it. I broke up your family. I hoped that after a long enough time, you could maybe forgive me. But it doesn't seem like that's going to happen. I don't hate you for it. If I was sixteen, I'd probably treat me the same way.

But the thing is, no matter how you feel about me, I love you. I care about you. I want good things to happen for you. I'm not your mom, but I care. I read your blog. In all honesty, I've been one of your readers for a little while. (Mostly the style section—don't freak out. I haven't been getting tips from you on how to make out with your father). But I know you; I know who you are and who you aren't. And you are not this person.

I know; I've given up many things in my life for the sake of being popular or beautiful or loved, whatever. I was a teenage girl once, too. Your father may not totally get it. But I do. I'm not judging you. But I do hope you will take

some time to reflect on who you are, and who you truly want to be. I love you, Leelee, and none of us wants to lose you.
Love,
Stacey

I reread the letter several times. And after time number four or five, I hold it tightly in my hand and start to cry.

28. HOW to LOSE Everything

Parents never ground you from school. It's sucky that I can't stay home, because the thought of going, of facing everyone, is making me legitimately sick. Sick enough that I really could justify staying home. Beads of sweat are popping up everywhere on me as I pull on my jeans, nausea roiling in my stomach as I slip my shirt on.

I can't do this. I can't. I can't.

But I have to.

I leave the house in silence, the kind of silence that weighs down my shoulders. The snow is deep, so I'm taking the bus. The day has already reached its maximum capacity for potential horribleness, so it's not like anything can make it worse, bus included.

I hunch my shoulders and look down when I board, trying to ignore the high-pitched squirrel giggles coming from the freshmen in the seats. I sit beside a kid who is always quiet, reading a graphic novel, because I doubt he gives a care. Then I plug my headphones into my ears and shut my eyes until it's over.

When the bus rolls to a stop, I follow the line outside. Slowly I make my way to the front door, take a deep breath, and step into the school.

It's like one of those awful dreams when you show up somewhere important, and you're naked. Everyone is focused on you, laughing, pointing, disgusted. It feels like every person here (faculty and staff included) knows about me.

"Hey, Renley!" I hear over my shoulder. I turn, shocked that someone is intentionally interacting with me, and find Sam. "Killer blog. I especially loved all the detailed accounts of the sexual shit you did with Taylor's boyfriend."

"He wasn't Taylor's boyfriend; he was mine."

"Was?" she says, raising an eyebrow. "So your outstanding prowess wasn't enough for him? Shocker."

Tears sting my eyes, and I fold my arms. "It was a blog. I never said anything on it that has the slightest thing to do with you. Why are you being so horrible?"

"Because you're fake," she spits. "And you're a nobody now. *You hurt my friend.* I'm Taylor's friend before I'm yours. Was that somehow not clear to you? And now everyone knows what a plastic little skank you are. Congratulations."

I swallow the tears down and turn around, power-walking down the hall just before she calls out, "And I want my share for that menudo and Sprite tip!"

I duck into math, open my mouth to talk to April, and she isn't there. But Mr. Sanchez makes up for it when he walks past my desk and says, "Sorry to hear you won't be joining us in New York, Miss Eisler."

Miss Eisler? What is this? Cooking? I feel a sharp stab of dread at that thought and pray throughout all of calculus and English that Seth won't be there either. He is.

I avoid looking at him, and when I near him, his jaw clenches and he blinks slowly, looking straight ahead.

"You're not gonna move seats?" I say.

He looks down at me. "You want to move, move."

And that's it. No helping me mix my ingredients, no laughing at my horrible attempts at flirting, no biting comments, even. Just sharp, quiet nothing.

By the time the last bell rings, I kind of want to throw up. I want to throw up in the bathroom alone and leave when the halls are empty and no one is snickering and whispering and knowing what I do with my tongue when I kiss a guy and where all the hickeys are that I've covered up.

I just keep my head down, though, and force my way through the line of people, and shut my door when I get home.

The next morning, someone has filled my locker with Sprite and disgusting day-old menudo and condoms.

The morning after that, I am a special report on the closed circuit school news. The lamest of the lame kids go out of their way to laugh at me. April still isn't in school, but that doesn't really register. Not right now.

Thursday, I fake sick so I can stay home, but Dad, newly decided to be an actual parent, makes me go, and

Taylor and Sam and Ash and Sophie make it their goal to ignore me completely, and everyone in the school follows suit, except for Gary Harding, who asks me to go out behind the junky annex and show him what I know about everything I wrote. I decline.

The week before Christmas break, sophomore year, is the first week since middle school that I've spent eating lunch completely alone.

☿

The next six days are awful. Like, horrendously so. It's Christmas, which means sleeping in and presents and cocoa, so it could be worse? But I'm mostly cut off from communication, so I've been left to wallow in the terrible situation all on my own. Surrounded by family, but really, when it comes down to it, alone. Dad has relaxed the texting ban, but I've discovered that even if someone does try to get a hold of me, I don't want to talk. And very few people are trying to get a hold of me anyway.

April, though, has called probably twelve times in the last several days, no exaggeration. And Drew puts that number to shame. The thing is, I don't know what to say to them. I've gone over it in my head so many times, and every time, I come up empty.

What do you say to the girl you basically screwed over so you could make out with a guy all night at a dance? I could have done that anywhere. What I really wanted, and I know this after 144 hours in solitary confinement, was for everyone to see me, looking like a sparkly Barbie on the arm of the hottest guy in school.

And, speaking of, Seth hasn't said a word to me, which is painful. I'm dying to talk to him, but I don't know how to. He feels completely betrayed, and he should. I aired all our deepest secrets to people I don't even know. For money.

The one who leaves me completely speechless and devastated, though, is Drew. What do I say? I'm still kind of angry that he ratted me out. And seriously? Some of those posts, he should have kept from my dad. But in all honesty, he was right. He was right and I was wrong and that sucks. I don't even know how to face him after some of the things I said to him a couple weeks ago.

So I just sit there, paralyzed. And turn on my computer.

Dear Readers,

As some of you (or maybe all of you) may know, my identity was outed recently. And I'm basically here to fess up and admit that yes, it was me. My name is Renley Eisler, and I started all of this to make some extra money, but over the course of blogging, I've given up a lot. Friends. Boyfriends. People I can't even classify. And not just other people . . . me. Everything I am, really.

So I've decided to give up blogging. I won't be answering any more questions from anyone. I'm not taking this down—I don't believe in erasing every mistake I've made. But consider this my fare-well from the blogosphere.

Thank you all for reading,
SweetLifeCoach -aka- Renley

After I post, it feels like a giant cement brick is lifted off my chest. It's over. That last week at school, isolation over break . . . It will probably suck when school starts back again—that awful invisibility, broken up with moments of extremely unwanted notoriety. But for now, I'm done. And so, when April calls for the thirteenth time, I feel like I can answer.

"Hello?"

"You're alive."

"Barely," I say. There's a long pause.

"Can you come over?" she finally says.

"I'll be there in just a few minutes."

I put on a new coat I asked for and received for Christmas and head out the door, now that I'm released from my grounding. When I get to April's house, that familiar nervous feeling is back. I knock, and her mother answers the door. The smile she gives me is not her usual smile, huge and genuine—it's small and forced.

"Renley. How nice to see you."

"Yeah," I say, hands in my pockets, looking anywhere but at her face. "Is, um, is April here?"

"Go on up," she says, moving out of my way, eyes holding little warmth. I walk slowly up the stairs and crack open her door. April doesn't look up when I walk in, and when I get really close to her face, I can see why. Her face is red and blotchy and her eyes are bloodshot. April never cries.

"Why haven't you been answering your phone?" she asks, still not looking at me.

"I was grounded up until a couple days ago. And I just . . . with everything going on with the blog and everyone hating my guts, I didn't really want to talk to anyone."

"Yeah," she says.

"But I'm here now. So, you know, yell at me about whatever you want to yell about."

She looks up at me. "About your blog?"

"Yeah."

"I don't care about your stupid blog."

I frown. "You don't? Then why have you been calling me and—"

"Ugh, Renley, not everything is about you. It's Christmas break."

I look at her blankly.

"Which means it's December."

Still nothing.

Her mouth falls open, and only then do I realize country music is playing softly on her iPod. April hates country music.

I gasp. "Oh no. Keith. That's why you were gone for that week of school and . . . I'm so sorry. I just completely—"

"Forgot? Yeah, I know. Well, he's gone now, so."

I fly over to her bed, knocking several pillows out of the way. "I am so sorry. I can't believe I forgot he was leaving."

"I can. You've been unable to think about anyone but yourself for the past two months. What does my brother matter? He's not making out with you."

"That's not fair," I say weakly.

She gives me a look.

"Okay. Okay, it kind of is . . . so he's gone? When does he get back?"

"Beginning of March." She looks halfway dead, hair scraggly, eyes dry and red. "But then we don't know where he's going. He could be stationed in the US or he could be sent to, like, Iraq. Or Afghanistan. Or anywhere. I just . . ." She draws her knees up to her chest and buries her head in them, then her shoulders start to shake.

I reach out toward her, then hesitate. Can I hug her or will she stab me? I've been the world's most awful friend since all this started, didn't even bother to call when she was out of school for a week, missed her brother leaving. But this is not about me. Screw it. I'm hugging her. I put my arms around her, hesitantly at first, then tighter, and she grabs me, too, and cries.

This doesn't feel normal, exactly. I don't think I've ever held crying April before. But it feels good.

"I'm sorry I wasn't here," I say.

"Me too," she says.

"When did he leave?"

"Four days ago. I shouldn't even be crying like this. But I mean, I miss my brother."

I nod. "Is that why your mom was being weird when I came in the door today?"

"Partly, but also because my parents don't totally love you right now."

That is painful to hear. Justified, but painful.

"I've been kind of a crappy friend, huh?"

"The worst."

I narrow my eyes at her, wishing she'd confirmed it with just a little less enthusiasm.

"So, are you still going to New York?" I ask, and her eyes cloud over slightly.

"Yeah. You better believe I am. I'm not giving up the trip of a lifetime just because my friend decided to crap out on me. I've been hanging out with Amy and Rory a lot anyway, and they're going. So it'll still be fun."

I try not to react viscerally when I note that she didn't say *best friend*.

"How about Cash?" I say past the lump in my throat.

Her eyes sparkle mischievously when I mention him. "Oh yeah. He's going. And that will be even *more* fun."

"I wish I could go."

"It's your fault."

"I know," I sigh. "Now I'm realizing how stupid it was, though. Like, what was I thinking? Giving up NEW YORK CITY to go to a dance everyone's excited about and then makes fun of later?"

"Super dumb."

We're both kind of quiet for a while.

"Are you and Seth still . . ." she asks, and I shake my head before she can finish her sentence.

"Nope. I mean, did you read the stuff I wrote? You wouldn't want to date me either, after that."

"He called me, you know," April says.

That shocks me. "He did?"

"Yeah. Yesterday. He wanted to know what I thought about everything. About you."

I swallow hard. "And what did you say?" I look away and clench my hands on my jeans, knowing the answer, not wanting to hear it.

"I told him that you were being completely horrible. Awful."

I deserve that.

"And I told him I couldn't even stand to think about you."

That, too.

"But then I said that you used to be my best friend for a reason, and that this was not you. And that you'd come around, if he gave you time."

"You did?"

"Yeah."

"What did he say?"

"Not much. But I think . . . I think you guys aren't completely over, if you don't want to be."

My heart flutters, something it hasn't done in a while. I stare at her, eyes wet.

"Thank you."

"I do love you, Renley." Her eyes are serious, not smiling. She doesn't qualify it, but I know that things are different between us now. Maybe not always. I hope not always. But they're cracked, fractured. And that's . . . okay.

"I totally love you," I say, on the raw edge of crying. And, for the second time today (which makes a first ever), I give her a hug.

Then I pull back and see that her eyes are still dull.

"You know," I say, "the blue in your hair is starting to go kind of green."

"Well, your highlights are black at your scalp."

"I brought some dye. I have it in my car."

She smiles then, genuinely. "Go get it then."

I don't even mind venturing out into the snow to get the dye. I'm just . . . happy. I have no clue if we're ever going to get back to normal, or if we do, how long it's going to take. But for now, we're alright. And I'm okay.

29. How to Figure Out Some Very Important Things

There is only one thing I can do tonight. One thing that I'm dreading doing. It has my stomach in knots and my throat all swollen and crazy and my pulse is through the roof. But it's something that, if I don't fix, I will regret forever.

So I procrastinate for several hours, like I've been doing for the past two days. I can't believe that after how mostly-well everything went with April, I've still waited two days to go talk to him. But it's, well, it's terrifying. It's more terrifying, though, to just sit here and do nothing. There's got to be some sort of statute of limitations on these kinds of things, and since he stopped texting yesterday, I fear I'm rapidly reaching that point.

So I throw on some clothes and crunch across the snow to his window. I pause for a split second, then take a deep breath, and knock. Drew slides the curtain back.

Doesn't smile, doesn't frown, just slides it and looks at me. It's fair.

"Can I come in?" I over-enunciate, hoping he can hear me through the glass.

He shoves the thing open and I climb in. Only then do I realize he is not wearing a shirt. Of course he isn't.

"I'm surprised you don't have a girl in here. Late at night on break and all alone? What's come over you?"

His serious face breaks into a smile, and I can feel every muscle in me relax, even if I know that relaxation might be short-lived.

"No, no girls. Haven't had any over in a while. Trying to deal with one of my many issues."

And there it is. Strings of muscle in my back all knot together again. He's not going to let me just blow past that night without some sort of explanation. And he shouldn't.

"We have something in common then," I say, sitting on his bed.

"Oh yeah? You finally giving up your love of screwing random girls every night, too? Good for you."

"You wish that was one of my issues."

"I kind of do."

I roll my eyes. "I've just been . . . working on things, too."

He sits down beside me, bed creaking. "Do tell."

"April and I got things figured out."

He smiles. "Good."

"And I stopped blogging."

"I saw."

"Cyber stalker."

He grins. "Yeah, maybe."

I'm so dehydrated at this point, I'm surprised I can tear up. But I totally do.

"I'm—" I choke on the words and have to steady myself. So I breathe, and Drew just sits there quietly, waiting. Then finally, I can speak again. "I'm so sorry, Drew."

He's still quiet.

"For that night. I can't even believe some of the things I said to you. Like, I replay it in my head and it's like it's someone else saying it. Did I really tell you you couldn't see past a giant hard-on you had for me?"

He shrugs, but then nods. "Yeah. I have to hand it to you, though. It was poetic."

I shake my head and sigh heavily. "I was totally horrible to you."

"Yeah."

"Do you even want me here?" I steel myself, preparing for the worst. Sometimes, there's only so much awfulness a person can love you through.

He laughs then, and I knit my brows together. It just seems so odd.

"You think I want you to leave?"

"Well, I was hoping not."

"You were awful. I mean, really awful. And I only halfway believe some of the crap you said to me that night, some of the stuff you wrote on that terrible blog. But that's not you now. That's not the you who's here, right?"

"No. No way."

"Then screw it. Now, if evil doppelgänger Renley shows up again, let me know, 'cause I'm kicking her out. Immediately. But you? I'd never ask you to leave."

I lean up against him then, head on his shoulder, and he takes my hand. It doesn't feel sexual, just comforting. He rubs his thumb over every crevice, lets his fingers slide between mine, then says, "You doing okay?"

"What do you mean?"

"I mean, I leaked some pretty vital information to some pretty vital people. Are you doing okay?"

"Yeah. I am now. I mean, the morning I found out, I was about homicidal. And my dad might never recover. EVER." I sit up. "Seriously, couldn't you have left the hand job post out when you gave him everything? I mean, come on."

He laughs. "That was a little harsh, I admit. I doubt he ever wanted to picture you doing *that* with anyone. Though, to be fair, I'm pretty sure he thinks we're doing a whole lot more than that. Or thought we were. Before, you know, everything."

"He did. You have no idea how many times I've had to correct that perception. With everyone."

"In a strange turn of events, I think he might actually like me now."

"Yeah. Apparently handing a parent sexual propaganda about their child does that for a guy. Who knew?"

"Maybe you should blog about it."

I smile into his chest and roll my eyes. "I think I'm good." Then, after a brief pause, "You know, it's ironic that my dad finally decides to like you *after* you're through being in love with me."

His thumb stops on my hand. "After what?"

"It's okay. I haven't exactly been lovable. I don't want to make things awkward; I'm just saying it's ironic." Something about actually saying it aloud makes it hurt worse than I thought it would. But the pain in my chest isn't going to change anything; I know that.

He turns my face toward his. "R, I have never stopped loving you."

My mouth falls open and I hesitate. "What?"

"I don't know how much plainer I can actually be here. I've been in love with you for . . . longer than I care to admit. And a couple months of you going crazy isn't going to change that."

"I don't know what to say."

"Then don't."

I can feel his pulse, hear his heartbeat, his chest warm against my ear, solid. And after what seems like forever, he says, "Do you . . . does any part of you feel the same way? In all honesty. I can take it. It's just, after our whole making out in my basement and what happened in the woods and, well, you know, my fragile man-heart is confused." He laughs.

I think for a little while. Here it is, laid out in front of me. Do I? Could I?

"If I'm being honest, maybe a small part of me does. But I can't."

He turns to face me. "Why?"

"You'd get tired of me after a while."

He sighs, irritated, and his nostrils flare lightly.

"I'm serious. Eventually, you would. What if I didn't want to sleep with you? Then what?"

He shrugs. "It doesn't matter."

I eye him skeptically.

"Okay, I'm a guy. I mean, *it* matters. But if all you want to do is make out with me until a year from now or until you're in college, or until we . . . like . . . get married, I don't care."

"Bullshit."

"Nope. And don't freak out; I'm not proposing to you. But I'm telling you it wouldn't matter to me."

"And the next girl who comes traipsing up to your door in her short shorts and spaghetti straps with her giant boobs, you would actually be able to resist that?"

"Yeah, I would. And I'd want to."

"And when I'm being crazy—"

"Renley. Listen to me. I don't care about other girls or screwing you or your weird habits or your crazy. If I say I want to be with you, I want to be with you. Period. I've said it before; I'm not your dad. But you know . . . I think I don't want to try to convince you anymore."

I stare at his eyes, not sure what to say.

"I'll always be in love with you. But I don't want to convince anyone to be with me. I think . . ."

"What?" I say, voice coming out quieter than I intended.

"I think I'm gonna let you go."

"What do you mean?"

"You don't want me right now. And I can't just sit here and wait for it. You don't trust me and you're terrified I'll leave you and whatever. Okay. You want to be with Seth. And that's fine. I'm letting you go."

I want to cry again. It's so stupid. Why do I want to cry?

"But I want one last thing before you get in your dad's car and drive off."

"What?"

His lips are on mine before I've had a chance to process—urgent, powerful, taking my breath away. And his hand is on my face, pulling it in toward him, so the kiss is deep and slow and amazing, and I can't even think.

But then he pulls back.

"I thought you said you were letting me go," I say, breathing shallow.

"Yeah. I am. But I want you to remember that he can't kiss you like I can. Remember that." He grins and pushes me lightly away. "Go."

And in a daze, I go.

30. HOW to BE ME

I walk across his yard, back to my house, mulling everything over. It's freezing out here, snow reaching up to my ankles, melting into my socks. I run into my house to grab a coat, and my dad catches me on the way out.

"Where are you going?" he asks.

"To fix something I broke."

He smiles and pats me on the arm in a weird display of paternal affection.

"Can I borrow your car?"

He hands me the keys and I run off. I jump in the car and start the engine, heart thumping hard. April said she didn't think it was over, but after everything that happened at school, I don't know how that's possible. She wouldn't lie, though. Not about this. I shouldn't be scared. I refuse to be. So I floor it and peel out of our driveway onto the little road, heading toward Seth's.

I can feel every bump in the road as I drive, and the closer I get to Seth's, the more confused I feel. I should be thrilled. I should be unable to think about anything else. Shouldn't I? When I'm about two minutes away, I can't make myself drive farther, so I pull off the road. Just for a second, just to gather myself.

Why am I feeling this way? Part of me is dying to get to Seth's door, dying to fix everything, or at least to try, to have his lips on me, his hands everywhere. But part of me, well, isn't.

When I let my head drop forward to rest on the steering wheel, it sets off the horn. It cuts through the sparkling quiet of the night and I jump back up. I have to make a decision. So . . . I do. And I turn back onto the road and drive.

When I get to his house, his car is not in the driveway. I frown, discouraged for just a minute. So I drive past it, to the only other place I can think of that he would possibly be. The only place he *has* to be.

When I pull up to our spot, his car is sitting there quietly, headlights shining off the overlook. My car is quiet, so I don't even think he notices when I park. I stop several feet back from him and walk for several seconds in the cold dark, then lean up against the hood.

Drew is lying there, hands clasped behind his head, staring up at the stars. They're phenomenal tonight. Of course he's mesmerized. But when I lean against the car, he turns his head toward me.

"You remembered a jacket," he says.

"Yeah. I'm a grown-up now, or something."

I hop up on the hood and slide over next to him. He doesn't move his arm out for my head. He faces the sky again. "That was a fast reunion," he says.

"Well, yeah. Probably because it didn't happen."

He's still staring at the stars, and I prop myself up on an elbow to look at him.

"No?" he says lazily. "Why not?"

"Because I didn't want it to."

He moves his head a fraction of an inch, then raises an eyebrow. "What? Afraid he wouldn't take you back?"

"No. I mean, I don't know. I thought he wouldn't. But after what April told me, I honestly think he might."

"So what are you doing here?"

"I told you," I say. "I didn't want it to work out with Seth and me."

He frowns. He's not going to get it, no matter what I say, apparently. So I slip my hand around the back of his neck and pull his face toward mine, meeting his lips with more intensity than I ever have with anyone.

He makes a low noise of surprise, but recovers in an instant, rolling over on top of me, car hood popping beneath us, slipping his tongue between my lips, and I just melt against him. His kiss is passionate, hard, possessive, and I run my nails lightly up and down his back, under his shirt. I can feel little goose bumps where my fingers trail, and he responds by playing with the hem of my shirt, tugging lightly at the hair of the base of my neck.

We stay like that for a long time—I have no clue how long—until finally, he pulls back from me.

"You..." he breathes, out of words apparently. "You... what? I don't get it. I'm not complaining, but you gotta tell me." He's running his fingers along the skin of my waist, giving me delicious chills.

"I was driving to Seth's house, almost there, actually. But I couldn't do it."

"Why not?" His voice is low and husky.

"Because I think for the last two years, I've just been scared. I can't handle the thought of losing you. Ever. And in all honesty, part of me still is, still doubts this. I can't lose you. Doesn't this make you feel . . ."

"Terrified," he says.

"Ultimately, though, I figured, if I'm with someone else, I have to give you up. At least part of you. And I can't do that either. I'm not willing to. If I have to choose, I'd rather be scared. Because . . ." I trail off and look away, but he gently pushes my face back to look up at him.

"Because why?"

"Because I love you."

He dips down to kiss me again, slowly, with so much longing it aches. But it's okay, because we can do this for as long as we want.

"I love you, R," he says, kissing me again, and trailing his lips to my ear and my jaw, and all the places Seth kissed that I know felt good, but never like this—like my whole body is on fire and bathed in ice at once.

"I've always loved you," I say again, because it feels right. Totally right. For once in a long time, something finally does.

Later, we lie together on the hood of the car staring up at the sky, not saying anything, because we don't need to.

He leans down to kiss me every couple of minutes, and I nestle into the crook of his arm. And when it gets colder, and the jacket I brought isn't enough, he sheds the layer he brought, and gives me his.

♂

"You're definitely imagining me naked now," Drew says when he strips off his shirt and jumps into bed.

I roll my eyes. "You think everyone is always imagining you naked."

"Most of them are." He winks. Totally insufferable.

This easy flirting—this coupledom—isn't as weird as I thought it would be. We got a couple raised eyebrows when school started again, the sex god and newly appointed social pariah. But it's good now. Weird sometimes, seeing Seth holding hands with Taylor in the halls again, and April hanging out without me. Not all the time, though. She and I are working on things. Still. It's different. But mostly . . . it's good.

Stuff with Mom is the same. And New York still isn't happening; I don't know if Sanchez will ever forgive me. But lying here in Drew's bed, watching the snow fall outside, hot cider on the nightstand next to me, it feels almost like nothing's changed. Like life is bizarre and crazy and twisted, but it's alright.

I wiggle under the covers and he jumps out of bed again, searching for the remote.

"Here," I say, and he tries to take the controller from me, brushing against my fingers very intentionally. And I hold on to it, so he pulls me up to kiss me, long and slow and unbelievably good.

Then he crawls back in beside me, and I lay my head on his chest, like I've done a thousand times before. But not *exactly* like I've done a thousand times before.

He flips through the channels. *"Twilight Zone?"*

I don't even know why he asks anymore.

Beyond it is another dimension. A dimension of sound, a dimension of sight, a dimension of mind . . . and the cheesy music starts to play.

I reach for his fingers under the blanket and he smiles lightly, then scoots closer to me.

"Hungry?" he asks.

"Starving."

"I'll order Chinese."

Acknowledgments

The making of a book is so the opposite of a solitary process. And there are so many people who helped turn this from a little cloud of an idea into a real, book-shaped thing.

Thank you first, to my writerly support and friends, who let me flail and panic and ask a hundred gajillion questions about a hundred gajillion things at all hours: Tabitha Martin, Sara Taylor Woods, Dan Malossi, Liz Lincoln, and Rachel Simon.

To the amazing friends of mine who read for me, and loved Renley and Seth and Drew and these words of mine: Darci Cole, Nazarea Andrews, Amy Reichert, Melissa Stevens, Jenny Kaczorowski, and Juliana Brandt. THANK YOUUUUUU.

Brett Jonas, YOU get your own line, you sparkly, wonderful, ball of encouragement. Drew loves you and so do I.

My online friends, writer buddies, book bloggers, readers, you guys are absolutely invaluable. Every last one of you.

Bree Ogden, THANK YOU. This book would not be a thing on the shelves without you.

To my incredible editor, Nicole Frail, thank you so much for your insight, and for loving Renley, and for championing this story.

To my friends, who believe in me and encourage me even when it means I have to skip out on stuff, and for just everything: Rachel Chase, Luke Chase, and Nicole Silvano. You guys mean the world to me.

My family, for believing fiercely in me and my stories and what I do. Special thanks to Papa and Nana, Mom, Chase (wordly partner in crime), Makenzie (thanks for teaching me the word "nocializing"), and Taylor (thanks for letting me use your name ;)).

Finally, huge, huge thanks to my little boys—Mal and Elias—for being cool while I held them on my lap with one hand and wrote with the other. And to my husband, Harry. Boy I fell in love with in high school, man I love today, thanks for being my Happily Ever After.

And thank YOU, reader. You are what this is all about.